AN UNSUITABLE DEATH

Lambert and Hook are on the trail of a sacrilegious murderer

When the body of a beautiful young woman is found on an altar in Hereford Cathedral, it appears that serial killer The Sacristan has struck again. But nothing about the victim is as it first appears, and Lambert and Hook have to solve one of the most puzzling cases they have ever encountered.

"Compelling characters"

Booklist

"A Clever Mystery"

Kirkus Reviews

AN UNSUITABLE DEATH

AN UNSUITABLE DEATH

J. M. Gregson

Severn House Large Print

London & New York

This first world edition published in Great Britain 2001 by
SEVERN HOUSE LARGE PRINT BOOKS LTD of
9-15, High Street, Sutton, Surrey, SM1 1DF.
This first world edition published in the USA 2001 by
SEVERN HOUSE PUBLISERS INC., of
595 Madison Avenue, New York, NY 10022

British Library Cataloguing in Publication Data

Gregson, J. M. (James Michael)
    An unsuitable death. - Large print ed.
    1. Lambert, Superintendent (Fictitious character) - Fiction
    2. Hook, Sergeant (Fictitious character) - Fiction
    3. Hereford (England) - Fiction
    4. Detective and mystery stories
    5. Large type books
    I. Title
    823.9 ' 14 [F]

    ISBN 0-7278-7023-8

Printed and bound in Great Britain by
MPG Books Ltd, Bodmin, Cornwall.

*To Patricia, a source
of inspiration over a
quarter of a century.*

One

Even in a secular age, Britain's medieval cathedrals inspire awe. Some of the people who work in them are no longer sure what they believe in, yet these massive stone monuments to a vanished age maintain their power over the imagination.

Emily Waters hurried into the centre of Hereford after depositing her two children at their primary school. On this bright August morning, she was conscious only of a fear that she might be late for work again, after the warning she had received last month. Yet when she rounded a corner and confronted the Cathedral, with its massive central tower soaring towards that heaven which had been so bright and clear for its original worshippers, the great building took her breath away.

Emily was a busy, unimaginative woman. Her reactions might well have been dulled by the familiarity of this daily routine. But with the sun behind the tower and the trees thick with the green of high summer, the scene still impressed her. Silently, she repeated to herself the well-worn platitude: this was a good place to be working, even as a humble cleaner. And she wasn't late. She smiled her relief as she hurried to collect her mops and brushes.

The choir had been here last night, rehearsing for the Three Choirs Festival, that musical celebration which moved among the Cathedrals of Gloucester, Hereford and Worcester, and brought a swell of pride to the breasts even of those local residents who never listened to a note of the performances. Kept the place on the map, they said. Reminded the country at large that these three cities had been here, and been important, long before some of the great modern conurbations were even thought of. This was the kind of sentiment which made people like Emily Waters determined that the Cathedral should be spotless for its triennial honour of hosting the Festival in a week's time.

The choir members wouldn't have made much of a mess, she thought. They were a tidy lot, on the whole, and they took their litter away with them. There might be a few chairs out of place, the odd hymn book knocked on to the floor, but nothing sticky spilt. And certainly nothing damaged or stolen; none of those awful depredations

10

which meant that the ancient house of God had to be locked against the sinful thefts and thuggish violence of the devil's modern-day battalions.

In any case, Emily this morning was to clean the altar and the brasses of the Lady Chapel, her favourite part of the building. Behind the high altar, at the back of the Cathedral, this beautiful bywater of worship was almost invariably quiet. The Chapel would certainly be deserted at this early hour, with the morning sun filtering wonderfully through the five great windows of stained glass behind the altar. Emily looked forward to a steady, rhythmical polishing of the brasses beneath the benign gaze of the Virgin, to an easing away of the tensions that were endemic to her busy family life.

She was so unprepared for the new presence she found on the steps before the altar that her first reaction was not one of alarm. This supine figure, as still and graceful as a carefully finished waxwork, did not at first carry any menace. Emily thought initially that it must be part of some pageant, some celebration of a particular feast. She was familiar with the children displaying their work within these high stone walls at Christmas and Easter, and her first feeling was that this was some

11

more adult version of pious celebration. It was a reaction which lasted no more than an instant. For this figure was life-sized, and too excellent a representation of reality to be even a waxwork. A girl, perhaps ten years younger than Emily's thirty-two years. Her face looked serene, with her eyes closed and her lips relaxing into the half-smile of a Gioconda. She lay on her back, with her hands clasped reverently in prayer across her breast, exactly in the manner of the carved effigy on the tomb fifteen feet left of the Lady Altar. Joan de Bohun, Lady of Kilpeck, died 1327: Emily, who had dusted that ancient effigy so often, knew the details by heart. This modern girl's hands were clasped in the same way, but the rest of the figure was much nearer to life than the stone one with the dog at its feet on the top of the tomb. The girl's dress fell in demure folds about her legs, falling away towards her small, shapely, shoeless feet.

Emily slowly crept forward with dawning realisation, set the back of her fingers with infinite, reluctant tenderness upon the un-furrowed brow, and found it as cold and unfeeling as any of the marble that lay around her.

Where always before Emily Waters had spoken in whispers within the confines of the Cathedral, she now screamed, and went on screaming until others rushed to her side and beheld what so disturbed her.

Two

People react to death in different ways. Police personnel are trained to take it in their stride, to respond to even such a bizarre death as the one discovered in Hereford Cathedral with calmness and intelligence.

Yet the men and women who staff the police service are human enough, as they are constantly at pains to remind those members of the public who expect them to be both infallible *and* pillars of moral rectitude. Murder brings a chill of interest to a police station, even in our own violent age. And there was no doubting from the start that this was murder, and murder of a particularly sinister kind.

The phrase that ran round the various CID sections of the West Mercia police within minutes of Emily Waters' sinister discovery in front of the Lady Altar was, "There's been another one!" Another, in other words, in a chain of murders, another one in the series of apparently motiveless killings that all police forces fear most.

14

Nearly always the serial killer is a psychopath who delights in making the forces of law and order look inept. Usually the victims are women, and nearly always the killer acquires a label which increases his publicity – such murderers are invariably male – and intensifies the terror the public feel. This man, who had deposited all four of his previous victims in quiet country churches, had been dubbed 'the Sacristan' by a media grateful for the evolving melodrama he was providing in the quiet news months of July and August.

Nearly always the serial killer selects his victims at random, and thus proves difficult to track down and arrest. The sorry tale of the bunglings committed in the hunt for the Yorkshire Ripper still looms large in the public mind as well as in CID instructional videos. And in the Severn and Wye valleys there are always the grim shadows of the awful Gloucester killings of Fred West to remind people of the depths to which evil minds can sink.

Within minutes of the death being registered on police computers, Superintendent John Lambert received a phone call from his Chief Constable informing him of the details of the time and place of the discovery. "It's another killing by this bugger the papers have taken to calling the

15

Sacristan. The first one on our patch. The Serious Crime Squad will be on their way there as I speak, but I'd like you to look in, John. See what you can pick up before the body's moved. I'll clear it with Billy Griffith."

Lambert sighed. He knew Billy Griffith, a heavy Welshman who had cut his teeth in the casual violence of Cardiff's Tiger Bay. They had worked together years before, when Lambert was a CID sergeant making his way in detection. "All right, sir, if you really think it's necessary. But they've already got the experience of the four previous murders to bring to this. They won't take kindly to a new boy muscling in."

The Chief Constable grinned despite himself at the thought of his grizzled Superintendent, veteran of many a murder investigation, being thought of as a greenhorn who might get in the way of the experienced team. "Just take a look, John. You're too old a hand to get in anyone's way. We need to be fully informed, that's all. The press will be on to me within the hour: I can guarantee that. If I can tell them John Lambert's been to the scene, that will keep them happy, for today at least."

Lambert smiled sourly at the vision of himself as a local celebrity. He was glad it wasn't his job to keep the press and the

16

other media satisfied. This was mainly a public relations exercise, then. He would show his face, pick up what he could to relay back to the CC, and then leave the formidable team already pursuing the Sacristan to get on with their work. But as he went out into the bright sun of the car park at Oldford Police Station, he could not suppress a small sense of exultation in his experienced breast. The instinct of the hunter, an essential property of all CID men, thrilled a little even now as he went to the scene of this latest in a bizarre chain of deaths. Already he was beginning the familiar routine of pitting his mind against that of the man who had perpetrated this strange killing.

Different profession, different reaction. The journalist who was on the spot within minutes of this latest revelation of the Sacristan's horrors did not disguise his excitement. Might make the nationals, this. Might even get him his own byline. To a man who had toiled for thirty years on flower shows and traffic accidents, the body of this young woman revived thoughts of the scoop which lurks deep in the imagination of even the most disillusioned reporter.

The Lady Altar was already cordoned off when Joe Roper got into the Cathedral, but he quickly assured himself of an interview with the finder of the body. Whilst Emily Waters sipped her cup of reviving tea, he rang his office on the other side of the town and secured the services of the paper's single photographer. Cathedrals were always photogenic. They'd have a shot of the North Porch and the great central tower, then one of the nave, then one of the transept as you turned towards the Lady Chapel.

The idea was to lead the reader onward into this solemn place, emphasising the appalling and sacrilegious character of a murder in such a spot. Even the roped-off Lady Chapel would be worth a shot, if they could include the uniformed constable who stood beside it. THE SENTRY OF DEATH, his headline over this section would run; Joe was sure he could get the fresh-faced young officer to adopt a suitably solemn expression for the camera. The lad's mum would be quite thrilled to see him standing in authority in this awesome setting.

Joe picked up a postcard of the Lady Chapel in the Cathedral shop: it might be worth superimposing an artist's impression of the corpse lying solemnly and shockingly in front of the altar of the gentle Mother of God. They said this killer rigged up his corpses to look like the figures on medieval tombs; Joe's quick eyes began to seek out examples in the marble effigies around him, which the artist could parallel in his impression.

Phrases tumbled like clothes in a washing machine round Joe Roper's active mind. THE SACRISTAN STRIKES SOUTH would make a good headline. This was the psychopath's first murder outside a tight ten-mile circle around Shrewsbury, fifty miles to the north. Joe would point out how this meant the widening of the reign of terror for the women of the West Country. It would be his duty to do it, he decided. Terror and sex always sold newspapers.

This was a young woman – he would get some telling details of her dress and any hints of disarray from Emily in a few minutes. No doubt the police would refuse to reveal yet whether this girl had been sexually assaulted, like the others. But he could make something even of that refusal, especially if he could get his artist to draw a short skirt and suggest a hint of interference in his impression.

And the Sacristan was getting bolder. He had placed his first three victims in the graveyards of country churches. The fourth had been positioned just inside the portals of such a church, by the ancient baptismal font. Now the maniac – that word must surely come into Joe's copy somewhere, but he would place it tellingly – had deposited his fifth victim in one of the high temples of the Christian faith, the ancient Cathedral of Hereford.

The contrast of madness with the solemn stillness of these unchanging stones would offer some splendid phrases for his columns in the nationals. Joe Roper made a note to brush up on his hazy notions of the history of this place, in which he had only once set foot before.

The body looked as cold and chaste as that of a sleeping nun. John Lambert wondered if it was the setting which had suggested this image.

The corpse had not yet been removed from its religious context. The Lady Chapel altar was about thirty feet wide, with pews in front of it. A notice at the point of entry read, *Here the Blessed Sacrament is reserved. Please keep this Lady Chapel as a place of quiet for prayer.* Lambert wondered if the awful irony of the words had appealed to the warped mind of the killer. More likely it was just the fact that this was the quietest and most remote part of the Cathedral, where his handiwork might remain undiscovered longest.

There were two wide steps in front of the

altar. The body lay upon the lower of these, between two six-foot-high candlesticks. Through the rich reds and blues of the five great panels of stained glass on this eastern extremity of the church, the sun threw globules of soft colour upon the unlined face. The limbs might have been merely resting, for there was no visible sign of how this woman had died. She lay on her back with her hands joined, arranged like a pagan sacrifice in this ancient Christian place.

But already she was surrounded by the lay business of detection. The police surgeon had been and gone, having conducted the brief legal ritual of certifying that this cold and motionless figure was indeed dead. The civilian fingerprint team were spreading their powder on the rails, the steps and any smooth surface which the murderer might have briefly touched. Soon the pathologist would begin his necessary assault upon the dignity of death to take the rectal temperature and search beneath the clothing for any supplementary clues about the context of this dying.

Lambert, so used to taking a central role as the investigation got under way, stood this time upon the fringe of the activity, an observer rather than a participant. He walked down the tiled aisle of the chapel,

21

passed the notice which said, *Visitors are requested not to pass beyond this point,* and stood at the altar itself. He introduced himself when the opportunity arose to the officer who was directing operations. "John Lambert, Oldford CID. It's on our patch and the Chief Constable—"

"Yes, Chief Superintendent Griffith said you'd be coming. Said I was to offer you whatever information I could. I'm Derek Cocker."

He was not unfriendly, had even afforded this tall, grave-looking man a brief smile. But his body language said that this was one more unnecessary diversion for a busy man with a major problem. He turned back to a survey of the dead woman.

From Lambert's height, Cocker looked small and lean, not much like a policeman at all. He seemed almost too short, but then to recruitment that had been waived since the time when a young PC Lambert had joined the force and trodden the beat. This man was certainly young for a Detective Inspector; Lambert tried hard not to resent the fact.

Cocker glanced at him from beside the body, remembered the wily old fox Billy Griffith had described, recalled his chief's old association with this man, and said as pleasantly as he could, "Come and have a look at close quarters, if you like. Not that there's much to be seen."

Lambert stepped on to the brown marble of the altar steps. He had to reject an impulse to kneel and pray, which burst through with startling strength from his childhood. Instead, he went down on one knee beside the corpse, studying the unlined young face, resisting an unexpected impulse to touch the skin stretched tight across the forehead. He said, feeling that he was stating the obvious but needing confirmation, "She died last night?"

"Yes, she's cold as mutton." The brutality of the younger man's language was an assertion of his familiarity with death. "The police surgeon confirmed it must have been last night. Perhaps we'll get something more precise in due course." His tone said that he didn't hold out much hope of that. The time of death was usually much more difficult to establish in fact than in fiction, and pathologists were more cautious than ever now that they knew their professionalism was likely be challenged in court. Usually the digestive state of the stomach contents in the post-mortem gave a fairly accurate idea of how long after the last meal death had occurred, but it would be up to the investigation to establish when that meal had been eaten.

"How did she die?"

Cocker looked at him sharply. "She was strangled. Like the other victims of this man." He was reluctant to afford the killer his label of 'the Sacristan', loath to afford this anonymous opponent the tabloid glamour of the appellation. He placed finger and thumb on the thin material and carefully drew back the chiffon scarf from around the slim neck, revealing the livid purple marks of violent death, the broad print of a thumb upon the point where the carotid artery had yesterday pulsed with life.

"Here?"

Derek Cocker shrugged. "Maybe. It would have been easy enough, if she had been taken unawares. She wouldn't have had the chance to make any noise. And this sign had been moved from the north transept to the entrance to the Lady Chapel." He pointed to a trestle with a notice in red capitals upon a white background which read, *Work in progress. Please do not proceed beyond this point.*

"Someone who knew the Cathedral and what was going on within it, then?"

"Or an opportunist who saw his chance of a little more protection. The sign was only fifty yards away. If he brought her here to kill her, or even brought her body here to dump it, he might just have seen the sign and used it."

A resourceful killer, cool in a crisis, however unbalanced his mind might be. Every one of the scanty facts seemed more depressing. Lambert reminded himself that this was not his case and tried to be grateful.

Lambert looked down at the girl. With her muscles relaxed into the tranquillity of death, she looked very young, probably younger than she had actually been in life. She lay on her back upon the marble floor, with her hands joined on her breast. He felt anger rising within him at this obscene parody of the image of serenity in death, as he saw how it echoed the figure on the ancient tomb to his left and many others of the carved marble effigies upon the Cathedral's tombs. "Do we know who she is?"

"Not yet. The other victims were all local girls, living within a few miles of where their bodies were discovered. But no one in the Hereford area has reported a girl who didn't come home last night. If she's a registered missing person, we should know who she is by the end of the day."

Without even thinking about it consciously, Lambert had set about establishing the policeman's automatic framework for suspicious deaths: who, how, when and where. He glanced automatically at the joined hands, at the slender, ringless fingers. In all probability, no distraught husband looking for his young wife. But this was a pretty girl whose life had been so abruptly halted. There would be a partner, perhaps, male or female – one had always to make that rider nowadays.

Cocker saw the older man studying the pale hands, hesitated for a moment, then remembered Billy Griffith's injunction that he was to give this old colleague all the information he required. The younger officer took a ball-pen from his pocket and carefully lifted back the unbuttoned sleeve of the girl's blouse. The flesh of the forearm was white and smooth for the first few inches. Then there was the mottling and roughening of the skin which every modern police officer has come to know, the result of hundreds of tiny needle marks. Heroin, probably: that was the most commonly injected drug. They would have to wait for the post-mortem to be certain of the drugs and the quantities.

In spite of himself, Lambert was shocked by the revelation of a modern decadence in this place that was so unchanging. He glanced automatically at the face, now so untroubled in death, wondering what agonies the mind behind that visage had gone through in its short life. Cocker said quietly, "The other arm's the same, and she's started on her thighs. She was a user, at least. Maybe a dealer. No doubt we'll know soon enough. That's probably why no one's reported her missing."

Lambert knew what he meant. It was not good news for any murder inquiry. A victim from that nightmare half-world of drug addiction, where people lived strange, desperate lives in the pursuit of their cravings. He felt a selfish relief that he was not involved in this investigation.

This was a world where violence was never far away. And a world in which the purveyors of that violence were too often able to remain both brutal and anonymous.

Three

Detective Sergeant Bert Hook had had an unexpectedly good result. He drove back into the car park at Oldford Police Station with a smile upon his broad and rubicund features.

He had feared that he might have to spend most of a stifling day in the Crown Court, but his case had been moved up the schedule because of the non-appearance of the defendant in the case above his. Moreover, the villain who had necessitated Bert's presence had pleaded guilty to armed robbery, asked for two other offences to be taken into account, and been sent down for a seven stretch. All in a commendably brisk thirty-one minutes. Bert, who knew at first hand about the law's delays and had found out during his Open University degree that man-of-the-millennium William Shakespeare agreed with him, was both surprised and delighted.

It wasn't until he got back into the CID section that Hook heard about the body in Hereford Cathedral. Police people being only human, a death as lurid as this one had the place buzzing with speculation. Bert was as interested as anyone. The Sacristan had killed on his patch; CID personnel can become intensely territorial about crime, and his arrival here was treated as if it were an attack upon their personal space.

Bert was glad to hear that the serial killer was the problem of the Regional Crime Squad, who already had a bulging but so far unsuggestive file on his activities. Bert's chief and friend, Superintendent John Lambert, had visited the scene of the crime at the behest of the Chief Constable, but that was apparently merely a matter of keeping the local force informed. Keeping the Chief Constable informed more like, thought Bert, so that he wouldn't look a prat when the radio and TV asked him to comment. Lambert was closeted with the CC now, they said, giving his report.

Bert set about using this last hour of the morning, when he had expected to be kicking his heels and waiting to be called for his evidence, to catch up on his paperwork. It was fashionable to deride that aspect of the job, and it could be boring, but on the whole Bert Hook didn't mind it. He had an orderly mind, a grasp of language that came surprisingly from his solid frame, and he liked to dispatch routine work that had to be done rather than let it accumulate. "Procrastination is the thief of time" they had taught him in his youth. And "Never put off until tomorrow what you can do today". Bert was a Barnardo's boy, and they had been hot on proverbs in the home.

He had been working quietly for ten minutes when he was told that a Mrs Rennie was asking for him at the station desk. Bert went thoughtfully through to the front of the station, where the public had access to their service, trying desperately to remember who this woman might be. Members of the public you had seen for ten minutes four or five years ago sometimes expected you to remember them instantly.

Bert didn't claim to be as good as some on names, but he rarely forgot a face, even when time wrought its inevitable changes. But he didn't recognise this woman. She was about forty-five, he conjectured automatically. She was tall and slim; she had an oval, rather wan face; its whiteness was accentuated by the absence of make-up and by hair that was straight and very black. She wore jeans and a long-sleeved navy blue top, its simplicity set off by a pewter pendant with a cross in a circular framework. The dominating feature of her appearance was an air of intensity. She gave the impression of a woman operating under either great stress or burning conviction, so that there was no time to spare for the social niceties most people use to grease the wheels of conversation.

She said, "You don't know me. We've never met, as far as I know. But I remembered your name. My daughter remembered it. You went to her school, to warn them about the dangers of drugs."

Bert smiled, hoping to provoke the reaction of a small relaxing smile in response. The pale lips did not relax. He said, "I did use to go round schools doing that, yes. Our officers still do it. But it's a few years since I was last in a school."

She nodded impatiently. "Seven years ago. That's when you spoke to Tamsin. When she was in her GCSE year."

"Yes. Most of the groups I spoke to were about that age. Unfortunately, the officers who do the talks now have to get in when the kids are younger, while there's still—"

"I think it might be Tamsin. This girl." Her dark eyes widened a little as if trying to fix him with their urgency.

"What girl, Mrs Rennie? You must excuse me, but I've been out in court this morning, and I'm not quite up to date on all the—"

"The girl in the Cathedral at Hereford. The one they found this morning. The dead girl." She delivered each staccato sentence

31

more abruptly, as if by the mere force of words she could galvanise this heavy man into action.

Hook said, "You'd better come in here, Mrs Rennie," and led her into an interview room. He prevailed upon her to sit down and went to fetch John Lambert, whom he intercepted fortuitously on his way out of the Chief Constable's suite.

Lambert took one look at the taut face of the woman sitting on the other side of the square table and dispensed with any preliminaries. He said simply, "I've come here from Hereford less than an hour ago, Mrs Rennie. I saw the young woman who was dead in the Cathedral."

"Has she been identified yet?"

"No. Not as far as I am aware."

"I think it's Tamsin."

"And Tamsin is?"

"My daughter. Tamsin Rennie." She spoke impatiently, almost angrily, as if so much should have been obvious.

"When did you last see Tamsin, Mrs Rennie?"

His catalogue of routine questions should have been emollient, were designed to take the edge off her fierceness. They seemed if anything to intensify it. She snapped, "I don't know. Not for months now. That doesn't matter."

"But what makes you think this might be Tamsin?"

"The kind of life she was leading, that's what. And she had digs near the Cathedral. Five minutes' walk from it, she said."

"Can you give us the address?"

"No. I didn't visit her there. Didn't wish to."

Lambert wanted to ask her a whole string of questions. Why had she not seen her daughter for so long? Had Tamsin been an addict? What did she know about this life Tamsin had been leading that her mother thought so dangerous? Why had she not sought to protect the child whom she now thought lay dead in the Cathedral? What did she know of the girl's companions and associates?

But any delay seemed cruel. Lambert snapped, almost as curtly and impatiently as the woman confronting him, "This dead girl may not be your daughter at all. I dearly hope for your sake that she isn't. But she's certainly someone's daughter. Are you willing to try to identify the body for us, Mrs Rennie?"

"Of course I am. That's what I came here to tell you."

"Wait here. I'll be as quick as I possibly can."

Bert Hook had more sense than to try to

make small talk with Mrs Rennie while Lambert made three urgent phone calls from his office. They sat together silently in the small, square room. Ten minutes later, he set out with that intense presence in the back of his police Mondeo to drive to the mortuary at Hereford.

The relative, if such she proved, could identify the body before the knives of the post-mortem got to work. It was kinder that way.

It was still not much after midday when John Lambert was called into the Chief Constable's office. Douglas Gibson, immaculate as always in his tailored uniform, was the confident face of the police service which the public wanted to see. His thinning hair was silvering now at the temples, but that was all to the good: people didn't want their senior policemen to be young or frivolous. Gibson's face and bearing said that he took all crime seriously, but was never baffled by it. Whatever his inner thoughts, his public persona said that he was confident that he and his men would win in the end.

Yet today in the privacy of his office he looked uncharacteristically ruffled. "You'd better hear this, John," he said. Then, as if he realised his anxiety had taken over from his normal courtesy, he glanced at the man standing on the other side of his desk and said apologetically, "I think you know Chief Superintendent Griffith."

Lambert looked at the deeply lined face of the heavy man who had stood up when he came into the room. Griffith had put on a lot of weight and a lot of age since they had worked together twenty-odd years ago as young Detective Sergeants. He wondered if those years had treated him as harshly as this man, three inches shorter than his six feet four but now markedly heavier. He wanted to ask how his old colleague had acquired the livid scar on his forehead above his left eye, which even hair brushed forward could now no longer disguise. Instead, he said, "Yes. Chief Superintendent Griffith and I go back a long way. Good to see you, Billy!" and shook hands warmly.

As if anxious to forestall any nostalgic exchanges, Gibson said, "I'm afraid Mr Griffith has brought us some rather disturbing news about the body found in Hereford Cathedral this morning."

"Aye. It sounds daft and all, but it's true. We're sure of that." Griffith spelt his name the Welsh way, without an s, and his native South Wales accent came out strongly on the phrases, as if his puzzlement had suddenly stripped away the veneer of standard English elocution.

There was an awkward pause and Lambert, trying to help things along, said, "I went over there this morning, just to keep us briefed. Spoke to your Inspector Cocker. It looked like another killing by this man the media have taken to calling the Sacristan."

"Aye, it did. But it wasn't. We're pretty sure of that now. There are differences, you see, with this one."

"But she was strangled. I saw the marks on her throat. And laid out in the same way as the bodies round Shrewsbury."

"Aye. Not exactly the same way, though. There are certain details we've never released about the other killings. The Sacristan – I'm calling him that myself now, to distinguish him – has always used an elastic band to keep the hands of his victims together when they were laid out. He winds it tightly round their wrists, so that it's invisible beneath the sleeves, but holds the wrists and the hands firmly together."

"And there was no elastic band used this time?"

"No. The little fingers of each of this girl's hands were tightly interwoven to keep them together, that's all."

Lambert said, "It's a small difference. The killer might simply have been in a hurry to

36

get away. The Cathedral's a much more public place than any of those he's used previously."

For the first time since they had shaken hands, Billy Griffith allowed himself a smile. It was a fleeting and mirthless one. "Yes, John. But there was no evidence of haste on that Lady Altar. The girl's body was laid out with elaborate care, with every fold of the dress diligently arranged; it even looks as if the hair was carefully combed back to make the effect intended. And there are other things as well. We haven't publicised it, but the Sacristan has left notes with each of his other victims. Obscene notes, handwritten, with spelling errors – we hope they'll eventually help to convict him. There was no note with this one."

"Anything else?" Lambert knew now what the implications of this were, but he might as well have the full catalogue of items.

"Yes. Perhaps the most significant of all. The other women had all been sexually assaulted before they were killed. And their underclothing removed. This girl had not been assaulted. And her – her undergarments were not disturbed."

Lambert smiled grimly at his fellow officer's hesitation. Strange what taboos death brought. The Billy Griffith he remembered had been notable for his lurid and uninhibited language and for a rampant sex drive. Now, in the context of murder and in a Chief Constable's office, he even hesitated to speak of the girl's knickers.

It was Douglas Gibson who said heavily, "So it looks as if we have a copycat killer."

The room was silent for a moment as the three heavily experienced men let the implications of this sink in. A second damaged mind turning to violence. A man probably as unhinged as the Sacristan himself. Perhaps bolder, for the Cathedral was a more outrageous and certainly a more dangerous place than any of the country graveyards and churches chosen for the Sacristan's killings.

And a man just as likely as the Sacristan to go on to further murders if he was not caught quickly.

In the small reception area at the mortuary in Hereford, Sarah Rennie gave her name coldly and clearly to the clerk at the desk. Bert Hook, standing behind her, realised that it was the first time he had heard her forename.

She was as crisp and seemingly unemotional on the rest of the routine information required from her, even delivering her possible relationship to the corpse she was to view as "Mother" without a tremor. Bert

Hook had seen a lot of identifications in a quarter of a century as a policeman. His first reaction to her control was a selfish one of relief. And he was well aware that shock took many forms, including an icy calm.

Somehow this woman did not seem to him to be in shock. Her directness, her imperious desire to dispense with the fripperies of social exchange, struck him as more a trait of personality, perhaps a little accentuated by the stress of this situation, than the effect of shock. She dispensed with the bureaucratic formalities as impatiently as she had dismissed every other obstacle between her and the viewing of this girl she seemed so sure was her daughter. Hook had more sense than to offer her the moment to compose herself before entering the viewing area that he would normally have suggested at this point.

The body's hands were clasped still in the pastiche of medieval marble in which they had been found, but the pose was now mercifully obscured by the all-covering sheet. Sarah Rennie's control held, even at the moment when that sheet was drawn gently back from the serene, nun-like face.

There was not even the sudden gasp of horror and dismay that Hook had thought was inevitable. Nor even the tears of relief that this was not after all her daughter. Mrs Rennie looked down at the tranquil face for a long moment, her eyes taking in its every detail. She was as calm as a woman contemplating the purchase of a piece of exquisite porcelain.

Then she said quietly, "Yes. That is my daughter. That is Tamsin Elizabeth Rennie," and signalled to the attendant that the sheet should be replaced.

Almost, thought DS Bert Hook, as if she had known all about this death.

In the brightly lit Hereford Council Chamber on that night of Thursday, August 18th, the meeting of the full council was almost over. One of the Independent members raised a point of order, and the Chair dealt with it painstakingly, anxious to show that his political allegiance was not colouring his reaction.

One prominent member was resolutely silent through the last hour of the meeting. As far as he was concerned, the important matters had been dealt with early in the evening and the important votes had been taken then. The meeting would have been concluded by now, if it had had a brisker and more ruthless person in the chair. Normally this member would have been patient, knowing from long experience that the more you tried to hasten things on in Council meetings, the more ponderous they seemed to become. Parkinson's law, the law of diminishing returns, and various other axioms were easily witnessed in local government, but Sod's law still seemed the most powerful one of all.

Especially, it seemed, when you had urgent business elsewhere.

He tried to avoid looking at his watch as the meeting wound its interminable way through Any Other Business. Had these buggers no homes to go to? Had they no life outside this place?

This last was the wrong question to ask of himself. It made him uncomfortably aware that a year ago people might have been asking the same question about him. Hopefully, indeed, most of them still did, for the thing that had brought his life alive could not be made public. Not yet awhile, anyway, she had said; not until he had sorted out her life for her and made things regular. Had that been allowed to happen, he would have been only too proud to announce their partnership to the world.

Whereas now, he thought bleakly, it must be kept secret for ever.

He fretted anew as the Chairman dealt ponderously with a question about refuse

41

collection in the new estate of houses in Tupsley. The Chair was too patient with trivia that should be referred to sub-committees. It seemed to be almost a principle of their operations that meetings had to be prolonged until after ten thirty, whether there were real items to discuss or not. Things would be conducted altogether more briskly when he was in charge. If he ever was.

He became suddenly aware that the Chair was referring to him by name. He gathered his resources, forced his racing brain into the strait-jacket of concentration, and referred the questioner to the decision of the Housing Sub-committee in their February meeting, which had been confirmed by the March meeting of the full Council. This stilled discussion, because he was the only one who knew clearly what he was talking about. Thank heavens for his memory, which had not let him down, even in this crisis. The Chair thanked him, gratefully and elaborately. Get on with it, you orotund old windbag.

It was ten to eleven before he had made his hasty farewells to his colleagues and moved away into the darker world outside. It was still warm on this August evening, but he wore his long winter coat and a hat, as he had not done for months. He did not know why he had chosen to wear them; perhaps he thought they were some sort of disguise, that if he enveloped himself in clothes he would be less recognisable. Well, it wouldn't be the first time that a man muffled secretly to the eyes had moved through these ancient streets, he was sure. The attempt at a grim humour failed to console him.

The streets in the oldest area of the city were narrower and quieter than the ones he had left. He was thankful to see that Rosamund Street was completely deserted as he turned into it. Yet the silence and the quiet made him also more nervous. He was relieved to hear the faint sound of a television set announcing ITV's news at eleven o'clock from behind one of the curtained Georgian windows beside him.

The high old houses on each side seemed to tower away from him, leaving only a ribbon of starless sky above him. The lamps which had been retained from Victorian times in this preservation area were picturesque, but they threw only minimal light upon the pavement he trod, with pools of darkness between them which more garish modern neon lights would not have allowed.

He should not be moving like a felon through these streets he helped to administer and control, he told himself. Yet he still felt obscurely that he was less likely to be recognised if he showed the minimum amount of flesh, so he shrunk his neck more deeply into his collar, and thrust his sweating hands deep into the pockets of his winter coat. He found the remnants of a packet of cough sweets there: it must be five months at least since he had last worn this coat.

It was a short street, but it seemed to take him a long time to reach the familiar entrance, to turn with only the slightest hesitation down the darkened steps that led to the door of 17a. He felt more secure in the pool of deep darkness at the bottom of the steps. He had got here without anyone noticing him or following him, he was sure of that. He listened for a moment, becoming conscious in that instant of how fast his heart was beating.

Nothing. No sound of footsteps, ringing or furtive, on the street above him. For an instant of blind, consuming panic, he thought he had lost the key. Then his fingers closed upon it at the bottom of his trouser pocket. In a few moments, he would be inside, would be able to remove all signs of himself from the flat, to wipe out any trace that he had ever been there.

It was what he had come for. What he knew he must do. What he had to do, to preserve the life he had built up for himself over fifteen years and more. And yet he felt his treachery as his trembling hands produced the key. He had come here so often with his heart full of love and his mind full of excitement. And now he was coming stealthily at night, with a heart like lead and an ignoble wish to remove all vestiges of himself from the place.

He knew it had to be done. It was what she would have urged him to do, his dear, dead, disastrous girl. His trembling fingers tried once, twice, three times to find the invisible socket of the lock. The key slid home and he turned it.

Four

On the morning after the Hereford murder, Lambert read what the press had to say of it over his breakfast. If you were going to be involved in a case, as he now knew he was, it was as well to know how the newspapers were treating it. And in due course, unless the culprit was arrested quickly, treating you.

The reporters didn't know yet about the nature of the Cathedral killing: they were still presuming that the killer was the Sacristan and smacking their journalistic lips with relish. **THE SACRISTAN STRIKES SOUTH** trumpeted the alliterative *Express* in two-inch-high headlines. The text beneath them informed a startled nation that, "Women all over the South West of England were last night taking extra care to lock and bolt their doors and windows against the maniac now universally known as the Sacristan. This latest and most daring of his killings has moved the goalposts of terror dramatically further south. Where his previous four killings had been confined to

46

women in the quiet country area around Shrewsbury, the Sacristan has now invaded the ancient city of Hereford. And there he has deposited the body of the latest and youngest of his victims in the medieval Cathedral, at the throbbing heart of that city.

"As shown in our artist's impression above, the body was left as a gesture of contempt upon the very steps of the altar of the beautiful seven-centuries-old Lady Chapel. No one knows yet when or where this innocent girl died. It seems probable that she was strangled within the sacred walls of the Cathedral itself. Police said last night that the body had been identified, but they have not yet released the details "

There was much more in the same vein, with some ingenious speculation about the sexual assaults committed on the previous four victims, which allowed the writer to hint that this latest victim had also been the victim of some awful sexual violation. The dress of the girl in the artist's impression which had been superimposed upon the photograph of the Lady Chapel was in enough disarray to reveal a shapely thigh, to support the implication that this girl had suffered rape at least before she died.

The article, which carried the byline *From our local correspondent in Hereford, Joseph*

Roper, concluded with an exhortation to the police from a vehement Herefordshire housewife: "For God's sake catch this maniac quickly. We cannot sleep safely in our beds, yet nothing seems to be happening. The police sit on their backsides and do nothing, and every week another innocent woman is killed."

The *Times* report was more sober, but its analysis of police bafflement was no less trenchant and rather more cogent. All the papers took the opportunity to exploit the photogenic possibilities of the Cathedral, with many expert shots of the massive central tower and a couple of stunning colour photographs of the Lady Chapel, with its brilliant stained glass backdrop to the tragedy. The *Express* was the only daily to carry an artist's impression of the body itself, but the *Mirror* had an aerial view of the Cathedral and its immediate surrounding, with a cross marking the spot where the body had been found.

Christine Lambert came and looked at the pictures over her husband's shoulder. "Don't they just love a maniac?" she said. "Especially in August when they are no politicians to get their knives into. This story could run and run."

"It could when they find out this morning that there isn't just one maniac, but two," said her husband drily, looking at his watch and turning with relief to the cricket page of his *Times*.

He felt his wife's hands tighten as they rested lightly on his shoulders. "Are you saying this latest killing isn't by this - this Sacristan?"

"I'm saying exactly that, I'm afraid, love." He went briefly through the reasons why the Hereford killing could not be by the same man who had perpetrated the four previous killings around Shrewsbury, as though he was reiterating them to convince himself as well as his wife. "The Chief Constable will be announcing that the Cathedral murder isn't the work of the Sacristan to the media at ten o'clock this morning."

"So you have a a Copycat Killer." She pronounced the phrase carefully, giving it capital letters, for it felt to her not a general phrase but a piece of the police jargon she had always eschewed in the days when her husband's preoccupation with his job had seemed to threaten their marriage.

He smiled at the way she produced the phrase. "Looks like it. On our patch, too."

The last words sounded like a warning in her ears. "But it won't be your pigeon, will it, John? Surely the Regional Crime Squad will be handling it." Again she produced the routine title with diffidence, as if any knowledge of police procedures or organisation would be seen as a weakness in her.

"We'll liaise, of course. And if this one kills again, it will no doubt pass to them. But they've got their hands full at the moment, not least with this Sacristan man, who will certainly kill again if he's not caught quickly. The decision last night was that the Hereford Cathedral killing would be treated as a routine suspicious death in our area. Douglas Gibson will announce to the media this morning that I'm now officially in charge of the case."

He tried – unsuccessfully, in Christine's view – not to sound elated by the fact.

Lambert took Bert Hook with him and went back to Hereford Cathedral. They left the Superintendent's old Vauxhall in the public car park and walked the five minutes to the Cathedral from there. As they crossed St Owen's Street, they saw uniformed officers moving in and out of the long line of shops, questioning the owners about anything suspicious they might have seen on the evening when the girl died. The routine of the murder investigation, the boring but necessary legwork which the public rarely saw and scarcely considered, was under way. By the end of the day, the

50

routine would have thrown up its normal quota of suspicious individuals and suspicious incidents, all of which would have to be followed up on the chance that just one of them might give a genuine lead to this particular crime.

Hook went off to check entrances and exits and the general geography of the huge building and its environs, whilst Lambert went to a prearranged meeting with the Dean of the Cathedral. The cleric was younger than Lambert had expected – how many times did he find *that* nowadays? he thought to himself wryly – a brisk and cheerful man rather than the austere Trollopian figure Lambert realised he had half-expected. The Dean was anxious to be helpful and found it difficult to conceal an indecorous excitement about the melodrama of murder within these massive and ancient walls. John Lambert was not surprised at that: he was well used to the charnel-house glamour of this oldest and worst of all crimes.

"This is an awful thing, Superintendent," the Dean said. "I shall not say like Lady Macbeth 'Woe, alas, what in our house?' though the press already seem to be doing so. It's an awful thing to happen anywhere."

"Indeed it is. And we don't know for certain yet that it happened here, of course."

The Dean raised his eyebrows above the blue, intelligent eyes. "You mean she might have been brought here after death?"

"It's a possibility. We shall have to consider it. We shall need to find out if anyone saw a man bringing someone who looked drunk or distressed into the Cathedral on his arm."

"Or her arm?" The Dean could not resist his amateur detective question. He then blushed incongruously at his temerity.

Lambert grinned. "Or her arm, as you rightly remind me. It would be easier for a man to bring a corpse into the Cathedral like that, for obvious physical reasons, but not impossible for a woman."

"It would be easier still to kill your victim here in the Cathedral. In the Lady Chapel, in fact, where she was found."

"Indeed it would. Especially if she didn't suspect she was in danger and came here with her killer when the Cathedral was closed to normal visitors. That's one of the things I wanted to check with you."

The Dean frowned. "It's complicated. Our last service is Evensong at five thirty. Once that is over, we begin to think about closing the Cathedral up for the evening. I'm afraid if you leave it open for very long after Evensong is over you get undesirables in." He looked suddenly defensive, as if he were wary of displaying an unchristian attitude. "It's all right encouraging sinners to come in and repent, but if they come in looking to remove your priceless silver that's a different matter." Then he grinned, refusing to be embarrassed at his practicality; a policeman more than anyone would surely see the logic of it.

"So we can say that by seven o'clock the Cathedral would normally be closed to visitors?"

"Normally, yes."

"Would it be possible for anyone to come in as a normal entrant and simply stay behind until the building was shut up for the night?"

The Dean frowned, considering a possibility he had not thought of earlier, fascinated by this new and intriguing business of detection. "I think it would, yes. The verger or whoever is shutting up for the night does a quick tour of the Cathedral before the doors are shut, but it's a big place, with lots of nooks and crannies. I'm sure someone who was determined not to be found could escape notice by hiding away in a side chapel or even just by moving behind one of our massive central pillars. If he was in the crypt, for instance, it's quite possible that whoever was shutting up for the night would simply call a warning to that effect down the stairs, if he was in a hurry." The Dean brightened with excitement at that thought. "And the crypt is right beneath the Lady Chapel, where the corpse was found on Thursday morning."

"Let's go and look at it now, then," said Lambert, and the Dean stood up eagerly to accompany him.

With the removal of the body and the conclusion of the work of the SOCO team in the Lady Chapel, the barriers had been removed and the area was once again open to the public. A dozen or so people stood at the back of the chapel, whispering to each other and pointing to the spot where the body of Tamsin Rennie had been discovered on the previous morning. Detective and Dean stood for a few moments in front of the altar steps, then went down the stone staircase to the crypt below.

The August day was warm outside, but this oldest and most atmospheric place in the Cathedral was cold and a little damp. The only light in this below-ground section was artificial. Huge stone columns supported the massive weight of the cathedral above the crypt. "You see what I mean?" said the Dean in a breathy whisper. "Your killer could have hidden down here, either with a body or with his victim still alive, until the Cathedral above was locked and

54

deserted. Then he could have gone back up the stairs and laid out the body on the Lady Altar where it was found the next morning."

"He – or she – could have done just that. But we can't assume that's exactly what happened. It's one possibility, that's all."

The Dean nodded. "If the killer hid down here – or even if he didn't, for that matter – why didn't he lay out the body down here? There's an altar here to satisfy whatever warped parody of religious ceremony he had in mind." He gestured towards the simple stone altar at the easternmost end of the crypt. "If, as you say, this man was a copycat killer, aping the crimes of the Sacristan, this cruder altar would be much nearer to the simple altar in the country church where that man left his last victim."

"That's a fair point," said Lambert, much to his companion's satisfaction. "There would have been less risk of the body being discovered quickly, and a smaller risk of the killer being seen with his victim. Perhaps he had always envisaged the tableau he set out for us on the steps of the Lady Altar. Perhaps it was important to his perverted sense of ritual that he set his woman victim upon the altar dedicated to the most famous woman in Christendom. Your question about the crypt will need to be answered in due course, but at the moment there's no point in speculating too far. Tell me, if our killer got himself locked in with his victim, alive or dead at that point, could he have got himself out of the Cathedral easily after he'd set out the body as he wanted to on the Lady Chapel altar?"

The Deacon looked suitably shamefaced. "Yes. Even on a normal evening, he could probably have got out. Most of the old doors at the smaller entrances to the Cathedral are very substantial, but they bolt from the inside. He could have drawn back the bolts and made his escape, I'm sure, especially if he knew the Cathedral well or had explored the possibilities in advance. But I'm afraid I've just remembered something which makes the question academic."

"And what is that?"

"We have the Three Choirs Festival here next week. There was a rehearsal on Wednesday night, in the nave of the Cathedral. There were about two hundred people in the place."

Lambert sighed. "So all the entrances were open?"

"No. Only one. But I'm afraid it was the most convenient one for your killer. I'll show you."

He led the way up the stairs from the

crypt, across the front of the Lady Chapel, and across the south-east transept of the great building to a solid oak door with a cloistered walk beyond it. "This is the St John's door. We shut all the main doors to the Cathedral but leave this one open, to allow the choir members only to get in through here. It's the easiest access for the disabled as well – we have three or four wheelchair people who enjoy singing in the Three Choirs Festival. I'm afraid, as you see, that it is also the nearest entrance for anyone going to the Lady Chapel." The Dean spoke apologetically, as if it were a personal omission on his part which had left this loophole for a killer.

Lambert smiled wryly. Life was difficult enough for detectives, without the complication of two hundred people rehearsing at the scene of a crime. At least there might be some witnesses to any suspicious behaviour. They could put out an appeal, if only they had any idea of the appearance of the person they were looking for. "We can probably assume that our killer came into the building this way, whether he came before the rehearsal or while it was actually taking place, and whether he brought his victim here already dead, or alive and unsuspecting."

The Dean shuddered involuntarily. He

had heard the great music of the choirs on that evening, soaring in the vast spaces to the vaulting roof of the Cathedral. Now he had to contemplate the picture of the killer, shielded from view by the high altar, laying out his obscene tableau in the dark serenity of the Lady Chapel whilst the sacred chords poured forth behind him. He said, "I'm sorry. I should have remembered the Three Choirs rehearsal at the outset."

Lambert shrugged. "It doesn't matter, I should still have wanted to look at the ground, and everything we said earlier still applies. The rehearsal just makes entry and exit that much easier for a killer, especially one who knows the building and its activities. You've been most helpful. I'll be in touch again if we need more information. In the meantime, you could keep your ears open for me among the Cathedral staff. It's possible they might have seen something they didn't realise was significant at the time, or which they think might incriminate someone they know. People talk more easily among themselves than they do to police on an official inquiry."

The Dean promised eagerly to help. He spent the rest of the morning in different sections of the building with his ears alert to the gossip of workers excited by the drama of the body in the Lady Chapel.

Now that the identity of the victim had been revealed as Tamsin Rennie, the ancient walls were full of speculation, and the Dean, licensed to eavesdrop by his role of assistant to the CID, shamelessly gathered as much of it as he could to his innocent bosom.

It was in the unlikely setting of the Cathedral Library, while the public queued to see the priceless medieval Mappa Mundi in the room next door, that he picked up the most startling piece of information. The bespectacled girl who worked amidst the Cathedral archives was so excited as she spoke to the girl on the desk that she could not control the decibel level of her whispering.

The figure laid out so demurely in death before the altar of the Blessed Virgin Mary had apparently in life been "quite a goer".

While the Dean was conducting his unofficial research, Lambert was comparing notes with Bert Hook on his way back to Oldford CID.

They were agreed that the killer, with victim alive or dead, had almost certainly entered the Cathedral by the St John's door on the south side of the Cathedral, since all other entrances, including the equally convenient but more public north door, would have been closed by the time of entry.

"What about access to that entrance from the town outside?" asked Lambert.

"Too easy, from our point of view," said Hook gloomily. "Two quiet old streets behind the Cathedral give easy access for pedestrians and vehicles at night. St Ethelbert Street has the Cathedral Junior and Nursery Schools and the Choir School on it – all places which are often busy by day but very quiet in the early evening, especially in August, when the schools are on holiday anyway. There's also St John's Street, which runs directly down to the back of the Cathedral past the Old Deanery. A quiet street, even more so in the evenings."

"How close could you get a vehicle to the St John's door?"

"Very close, unfortunately. There's an extensive House Yard adjacent to that door, behind the Cathedral. It's not a public parking place, but it's not manned and you certainly wouldn't be challenged if you drove into it in the early evening. By day it would be filled by the cars of people who work in the Cathedral, but in the evenings there would be plenty of room."

"That might be to our advantage, if we can find anyone who was around. A lone car stays in the memory much more than one anonymous in a full car park."

Hook shook his head glumly. "On most evenings, you'd be right, but there was this damned rehearsal for the Three Choirs Festival next week. Choir members who knew of the existence of the House Yard park are sure to have used it."

"True. We'll have to try to find anyone who witnessed the departure of a vehicle while the rehearsal was still in full swing. Of course, we still have no idea whether the body was brought there in a car or van. Or whether the victim and her murderer walked into the Cathedral, either separately or together." They were thoughts which completed the gloom and emphasised how they were still at the very beginning of the investigation, twenty-eight hours after the body had been found and around forty hours after the murder had been committed.

The Chief Constable, Douglas Gibson, was scarcely more cheerful at the midday conference he called for the newly constituted CID team. "The media boys were delighted to find out from me this morning that we have not one but two maniacs at large. They'll make the most of that and then go to town as usual on police bafflement. 'Copycat Killer' will be all over the headlines tonight and tomorrow. What's

61

more, they quizzed me about the implications of that."

There was silence in the crowded room. They knew what he meant. Copycat killers were the worst of all from the police viewpoint. They meant that all the information in the dossier already compiled on the original serial killer – the Sacristan in this case – was useless for this new murderer. And a man imitating the methods of another left less of himself at the scene: there would be little information and a wide range of suspects, as there never was in the family murders which made up three-quarters of the homicide statistics.

It was the Chief Constable who concluded his briefing of the team with the worst thought of all: "You must bear in mind that copycat killers are as likely to be psychopaths as the serial killers they choose to imitate. That makes them just as prone to kill again, if they are not caught quickly."

Five

By three o'clock on that Friday afternoon, house-to-house enquiries in Hereford had revealed the address of the dead girl. By four o'clock, Lambert and Hook were ringing the bell of the three-storeyed terraced house.

17 Rosamund Street was a fine, large house which had come down a little in the world, so that its windows had a variety of ill-matched curtains and the once handsome front door was scratched and in need of paint. It was a solid enough barrier, however, and they heard no sound from behind it until it opened abruptly and an alert but rather squat woman of about forty confronted them. "Mrs Jane King? We're here about the murder of Tamsin Rennie," said Lambert, showing his warrant. "I'm Superintendent Lambert and this is Detective Sergeant Hook."

"I've already spoken to the police this afternoon," she said resentfully. "I said all I've got to say to the lad in uniform."

"Really? Well, you'll need to say it all

63

again to us, I'm afraid. And to answer whatever questions DS Hook and I might find to put to you. Do you want to do it here on the step or somewhere more comfortable?"

Jane King looked at him evenly for a moment, as if measuring an adversary. Even with the advantage of the substantial stone doorstep on her side, her blue eyes were still a little below the cool grey ones which studied her face so unblinkingly. Then she said, "I suppose you'd better come in," and led them through a rather cluttered hall, with a wheelchair and an old-fashioned hatstand, and into a surprisingly comfortable ground-floor sitting room at the back of the house.

She gestured without a word at a chaise-longue, and the two big men sat stiff and upright, facing a low Georgian window, through which they could see a neatly clipped lawn and a garden where roses climbed the wall behind a bed of bright red geraniums and light blue lobelia. It was an enclosed area which had probably not changed much in two centuries.

Lambert said without preamble, "Tamsin Rennie was murdered. You've probably heard or read about where her body was found. We know very little about her, as yet. We're here to remedy that situation. No doubt as a responsible member of the public you will be anxious to assist us."

Jane King's face showed no reaction. She was sitting forward, as unrelaxed as they were, on an elegant matching armchair. She wore navy trousers and a short-sleeved lighter blue silk blouse. She was lightly made up, but what cosmetics she wore had been carefully applied to the rather square face beneath the short dark hair. Lambert wondered if, despite her grudging attitude, she had known all along that she would sit here at some time and talk to men like them.

She said, "I warn you, I don't know much about the girl. She paid her rent on time and didn't cause any trouble. If they do that, I don't want to know much about them. They're entitled to their privacy."

" 'They' being your tenants? You let rooms?"

"Yes. Six bedsits and a small basement flat."

"And Tamsin Rennie had one of the bedsits?"

A moment's hesitation. "She did when she first came here."

"Which was when?"

"About eighteen months ago."

This was rather like drawing teeth. "But she wasn't living in one of your bedsits at the time of her death?"

65

"No. She moved into the basement flat. Eleven months ago."

They noted the precision of that. "Presumably the rent for that is higher than for the bedsits?"

"Yes. I charge almost twice as much for it. It has a separate bedroom and kitchen. And before you ask me, I don't know where her money came from. She didn't tell me and I didn't ask. I told you, so long as my tenants obey my rules, they're entitled to their privacy."

"An admirable system, I'm sure. But not very helpful to harassed policemen, in these circumstances."

If she detected his irony, she did not choose to register it. Instead she said stiffly, "One does not envisage such circumstances when setting up a system."

"Why didn't you come forward and say the girl lived here, Mrs King? Her body was found not five hundred yards from here. Her identity was released last night."

"I was away yesterday. Visiting a friend in Cardiff. I didn't know it was Tamsin until I heard the name on the television news this morning."

Did the reply come a little too pat, as though it had been prepared? Of course, it might be information she had already given to the uniformed man who had come here earlier, but he doubted that: the young officer would scarcely have asked her about her movements on the previous day; he would have been too eager to radio in with the news of his discovery of the victim's address. And even this morning, when the girl's identity had been announced, Jane King hadn't come forward; it had been the house-to-house that had revealed where the girl had lived, at about three o'clock. Lambert did not follow up her absence in Cardiff; the woman was merely helping the police voluntarily with their enquiries, and could easily become even less cooperative. Instead, he let the unspoken query hang in the air between them in a moment of silence. Then he said, "When did you last see Tamsin Rennie?"

Jane King allowed her face to relax into a smile, so that it became immediately more attractive. "Alive, you nearly added, didn't you? Well, just to satisfy you on that one, I haven't seen the poor girl dead; nor have I any idea who killed her. The last time I saw her was on the day of her death, at around ten on Wednesday morning. I can be so precise because I've already been through it with the uniformed lad who came here at lunchtime." She was confident, almost amused; her blue eyes seemed to mock the futility of this routine, repeated question.

"How do you know the day she was killed, Mrs King?" Lambert could play games too, if it disconcerted his subject.

For a moment, there was a gratifying degree of alarm in those revealing blue eyes. "Well, surely, if she was found—"

"She was found yesterday morning. There was no revelation in any of the accounts that she had died on the previous evening. We haven't yet released the time of death."

Her smile had disappeared abruptly, but it didn't take her long to recover some composure. "Well, it must have been implied in the accounts I read that Tamsin had been dead overnight. They said she was found in the Lady Chapel of the Cathedral, laid out ready for discovery like one of those carved effigies on the medieval tombs in there. I assumed she'd been killed on the previous night and left there."

"Well, you assumed correctly. We don't know precisely when she died yet, but it was certainly some time on Wednesday night." Lambert smiled a little, watching her relax. "Where were you on Wednesday night, Mrs King?"

Placed where it was, the question came almost like an insult, and the square face flashed with anger for an instant. "I was out for dinner. With friends, on the edge of the town. I can give you their names and phone number. If you think it's really necessary."

"Oh, I do. And we'd better have the address as well, please. The more people we can eliminate early from this inquiry the better, as I'm sure you'll appreciate."

The last sentence was conciliatory, and she accepted it as such and gave the details readily enough to Bert Hook, who recorded them in his round, rather slow hand on a new page of his notebook. By the time he had done so, she was drumming her fingertips impatiently on the arm of her chair, but Hook added his own, unexpected query, "And what time would you say you arrived at the house of Mr and Mrs Fraser, Mrs King?"

"Oh, I couldn't be precise. I didn't expect to be questioned about it by the CID, did I?" Her attempt at a sardonic laugh was not a success. "About twenty past seven, I should think. You could check it with the Frasers, I expect."

Lambert said abruptly, "You must forgive me for mentioning this, but you may understand that I have to. You do not seem to be very much upset by this death."

She was startled more by his directness than by the question itself, for which she had evidently been prepared. "I didn't know the girl well. As I say, my view is that my tenants are allowed their privacy. If I see

69

anything of their comings and goings, it is by accident rather than design. And Tamsin Rennie had the basement flat, with its own entrance, even its own number, 17a. I saw even less of her than the others."

"So you won't be able to tell us much about her lifestyle? You understand that in a murder case the first thing we have to do is to build up a full picture of the victim. That is especially important when the death does not appear to be one of those murders within a family which, as you may know, are very common."

"I understand. I can't help you, that's all." She looked as though that thought gave her some satisfaction.

"Do you know where she worked?"

Jane King hesitated, as if wondering whether to regard even this as some sort of assault upon her autonomy. "She worked at Brown's Bookshop, last I heard."

Lambert knew it. It was a rather appealing old shop which dealt mainly in second-hand books, about half a mile from this house. "Thank you. I wouldn't have thought that her salary there would pay the rent of your flat."

"I've told you, that wasn't my concern. It wasn't up to me to ask her where the money was coming from when she paid her rent, was it?"

"Indeed it wasn't. It's just that it would have been useful, now that she's been killed, if you had known where the extra money was coming from."

"Well, I don't. Perhaps her parents were helping her out."

"I doubt it, Mrs King. There seems to been some sort of domestic rift. Her mother didn't even know exactly where she was living."

She shrugged. "A lot of them leave home because they can't stand it there. They're better off here than on the streets, aren't they?"

"Indeed they are. If they can afford it, without breaking the law to raise the rent."

The blue eyes were wary, meeting his challenge, watchful for any assault upon her air of invincible ignorance about the activities in the life of this girl, who had become so troublesome in death. "No one who lives here breaks the law, not that I'm aware of."

"But as you say, you might very well not be aware of it. You make it a policy not to ask questions, not to find out too much about the lives of your tenants."

"I told you: they're entitled to their privacy." She was repeating it doggedly, like a piece of dogma from which she could not afford to deviate.

Lambert studied her for a tiny, insulting moment. "What would you say if I told you that Tamsin Rennie was a drug user?"

She raised her eyebrows high above the clear blue irises. "I'd say I was surprised. But only mildly, I suppose. They tell me that pot is commonly smoked among the young nowadays. Some people even say that the police turn a blind eye to it." She smiled, like one who had scored a small but definite point in an amusing game.

"We're not talking about cannabis here. We haven't had the full post-mortem results yet, but I'd be pretty sure myself that Miss Rennie was a hard drug addict. Probably heroin, but we shall know soon enough."

"You surprise me. But then, I wouldn't know the symptoms to look for like a police person, would I? And I told you, I had very few dealings with the girl. If I'd known about this, she'd have been on her way."

"I see. Well, you will no doubt know enough about the subject to be aware that it isn't a cheap habit. It makes it even more difficult at this moment to see where she got enough money both to support this habit and to pay her rent."

"And I've already told you that I know nothing about that."

"You have. We shall need to find out the facts, in due course, though. It may well prove to have something to do with her death."

Jane King's shoulders shrugged beneath the silk blouse. She seemed to be at pains to indicate that the matter was of supreme indifference to her. "I've no idea where her money came from."

"Did she pay her rent by cheque?"

Her eyes narrowed and she said, "I can't remember at the moment. I have seven different sources of rent in this house, you know." Lambert wondered if she was calculating the odds of discovery; they could find out if the cheques had passed through her bank account, if she became a suspect at a later stage. But he couldn't see why that should happen. Eventually she said, "Once or twice in the early days she gave me a cheque. In the last few months, it's always been in cash."

"New notes or used ones?"

"I really can't remember. Used ones, I think. In tens and twenties."

Precise that, for someone who couldn't remember. "Thank you. Can you recall any regular visitors to that basement flat in the last few weeks? I needn't stress the importance of this: it's obvious we shall need to investigate anyone who was in regular contact with Tamsin, now that she's become a murder victim."

She thought hard for a moment, then shook her head. "I'm sorry. I can see the importance of the question. But one of the things my tenants pay for is their privacy. The kind of woman who watches their every move from behind lace curtains wouldn't be a very popular landlady."

Lambert smiled. "No. Old ladies who have nothing better to do all day than spy on their neighbours from behind lace curtains are not usually popular with anyone. Except policemen, of course. I've come across quite a few useful busybodies in my time." He rose to his feet and Hook followed him, shutting his notebook carefully, conveying that impression of bovine stolidity which had caught many a villain off guard.

"I'll ask my other guests if they know any more than I do when I see them."

"Please do. Other members of our team will wish to question them, too. And we'll need to get a Scene of Crime team into that basement flat to go over it very thoroughly. I'm afraid you won't be able to re-let it until we give you clearance."

She smiled. "That won't be a problem. As it happens, the rent was paid until the end of September. I'm quite prepared to give a rebate to the next of kin. And I may not be a demonstrative woman, but I liked what

74

little I saw of Tamsin Rennie. I hope you get the swine who did this to her."

Jane King's knowledge of the movements and contacts of her basement tenant were irritatingly minimal, thought Lambert, as they drove away from the high, spacious Georgian house. Her ignorance appeared genuine enough, but he would postpone judgement on that for the moment.

It was Detective Inspector Chris Rushton who attended the post-mortem examination on Tamsin Rennie.

He had undertaken such tasks many times before, but he was moved and depressed despite himself by the slow ritual of examination conducted over the young corpse, flawless apart from the marks of repeated drug injections on both arms and one of the thighs. Curiously, these minor imperfections seemed only to emphasise the perfection of the body as a whole and the pity of this death.

The photographs taken between the removal of each item of clothing, the removal of the earrings from the pierced ears, the fingernail clippings and scrapings dropped into the labelled plastic bags, the sampling of the girl's thinly applied lipstick to match against any smears which might later be found upon her assailant's clothing, the Sellotaping of the blackened area around her throat to lift any minute traces of material left from the gloved hands of her strangler, the sampling of the genital area for any traces of semen, all seemed like assaults upon the privacy of a defenceless and beautiful young woman.

They would have to wait for the morrow for the full written PM report, which he would feed into his computer with the other information accruing from the efforts of the thirty-man team already allotted to the murder. But what he learned at the scene of the autopsy did not add much to what they already knew. The girl had died by strangulation. Probably she had been surprised and it had happened too quickly for her to defend herself, for there did not seem at first glance to be any skin or hair trapped beneath her nails. There was no trace of sexual assault, though the girl had been sexually active in the months before her death.

To some effect, apparently. That was the one new and potentially useful piece of information DI Rushton carried away from the Hereford autopsy.

Tamsin Rennie had been two months pregnant.

Six

Murder hunts do not cease at weekends. The majority of the team of thirty carried on with the dull but necessary routine of the investigation, patiently trying to contact anyone who had seen Tamsin Rennie in her last hours.

The investigation of the occupants of the house where she had lived out the last months of her life proved disappointing. Sergeant Jack Johnson and his SOCO team turned up very little which seemed significant in the basement flat she had occupied. There were a couple of empty syringes, but no supply of heroin. Not many clothes, but the ones the single wardrobe contained were expensive. There was nothing to suggest how this girl with what must have been a modest salary from a bookshop had been able to afford either these clothes or the rent of this well-furnished, spacious flat.

There were four women and two men who rented the six other rooms in the high Georgian house. The youngest was twenty-three, the oldest was forty. All of them seemed to regard their residence there as temporary, though their notion of temporary varied. None of them knew much about the girl who had lived in the basement. Or none of them was admitting to knowing very much: the police officers who interviewed them made that reservation with professional scepticism.

Two of them had seen an older man visiting Tamsin's flat. Whether it was the same man, whether it had been an isolated visit or one of a series, neither of them could say. There had been a younger man too. They thought he had visited more regularly, but no one was sure about how often. They thought it was the same young man on several occasions, but when they were questioned about his appearance it emerged that they could not even be sure of that.

Jack Johnson came to report the findings of the SOCO team to Lambert. They were old hands together, these two, and the grizzled Sergeant was quite apologetic about the series of blanks he had drawn. "I had a word with whoever was around in the place while the team were examining the flat, but I didn't find out much about the girl. I got the impression that some of those people knew a little more than they were telling me. Not much perhaps, but a little. They all seemed to want to give me the bare facts and draw the line at any speculation."

"And you say the flat was tidy?"

"Too tidy, if you ask me. Especially for a heroin user. There were clean sheets on the bed, clean smalls in the drawers. The floor looked as if it had just been vacuumed. We've bagged everything we could, and the lads picked up one or two outside fibres from the carpets and the chairs, but I doubt if anything will prove to be very useful."

"Do you think someone had been there before you?"

Johnson pursed his lips, almost as reluctant to commit himself as if he had been in court. It was this habit of caution which made him an excellent Scene of Crime Officer; his teams found him irritatingly slow at times, but his methodical approach and refusal to cut corners meant that very little was missed. "I think someone had been over that place since the girl was killed. Couldn't say who. We don't know how many keys there were. There's only a Yale lock on the basement flat. Mrs King has one herself and gave one to Tamsin Rennie. As she points out, there is no guarantee that the girl didn't have other keys cut. I gave her the go-ahead to get a new lock fitted, by the way."

A sensible measure, with a murderer possibly at large with a key. Lambert said,

79

"What did you make of Mrs Jane King?"

"A shrewd woman, who wasn't giving much away. I had the feeling she might know rather more than she was telling, but I couldn't be sure of that. It may be just that she keeps herself to herself and expects others to do likewise. She kept going on about respecting their privacy."

Lambert smiled. The same phrase she had repeated with him and Bert Hook. He couldn't see the resolutely methodical Johnson getting much more information than she wanted to give from the composed and alert owner of that rambling house. "Do you think Jane King had been in and cleaned the flat and removed anything that might have been useful to us?"

"She said not. She said Tamsin was a clean and tidy girl, or she wouldn't have allowed her to rent the best accommodation in her house. Pointed out the vacuum cleaner to us in a cupboard. There was nothing to analyse there, by the way: it had a clean bag in it. I've got people investigating the contents of the dustbin bags from the house, but I'm not hopeful. If it was someone from outside the house who went through the flat and cleaned it, he would surely have taken the stuff away with him."

"Did the other tenants have any views on Jane King?"

"Not so's you'd notice. They almost put up the 'No comment' signs when she was mentioned. Perhaps they just don't want to offend Mrs King and risk losing their rooms. Those bedsits are surprisingly spacious and well furnished." Johnson spoke as an expert who had seen many hundreds of rented rooms, sordid and salubrious, in his time.

Lambert frowned. "We're not finding enough out about the murder victim, so far. I was hoping you'd pick up more from that flat."

"Sorry, Guv'nor. I've not come across many places that had less to offer." Johnson looked glum, then dived suddenly into his black briefcase, like a conjuror producing the rabbit after all for a disappointed audience. "They probably won't lead us anywhere, but there were just two photographs. They were between two folded blouses, in the top drawer of the dresser in the living room."

Lambert took the pictures, each encased in clear polythene, like everything else the SOCO team had removed from the flat. A man who looked to be in his mid to late forties, smiling straight at the camera in a studio portrait, his chin lifted a little to disguise his receding hair. And a colour picture of a younger man, good-looking in a rather gaunt way, taken in striking profile against what seemed to be black velvet.

A strangely contrasting and as yet anonymous pair. He wondered what part each had played in the young life of Tamsin Rennie. And whether either of them could have been the man who ended that life so harshly.

At Brown's Bookshop, DS Hook was not finding out much more about the dead girl than the Scene of Crime team at her residence.

The owner of the bookshop, Cedric Brown, was in his late fifties, grey haired, worried, and with a slight stoop. "Miss Rennie came to work here about a year ago. I was willing to train her up in the trade. The business didn't really warrant an assistant, to be honest with you, but I was trying to look forward a few years to the time when I retire. My wife thought that if we got someone suitable we could leave them to manage the place and just take a little out of the business to supplement our pensions. We were both civil servants, you see, until five years ago."

Bert Hook did see. Another man who had always wanted to run a bookshop, had wanted to live his life surrounded by the objects he loved, who had persuaded his wife to retire early with him to do the thing they had always wanted to do. And who had no doubt found it much harder to wring a living from this rather old-fashioned shop at the wrong end of the town than he had expected.

The space for new books, hardback and paperback, was cramped, so that the easy sellers could not be strikingly displayed. Over half the shop was given over to second-hand books. Bert wished he had time to browse there, made a note to come back when he was not on duty to see if he could add to his collection of cricket literature. But he was willing to bet that more browsing than buying went on in the second-hand section – and even that this pleasant, helpful man was happy to indulge the browsers.

"Was Tamsin Rennie a satisfactory employee?"

Brown looked for a moment as if he was reluctant to speak ill of the dead. Then he shook his head sadly and said, "I'm afraid not. She was interested in books, and in the first few weeks she learned quite a lot. She even taught me a few things – largely about what our computer could do. She helped me to streamline our ordering system. And for about three months she was quite a pleasure to have around: bright and interested, and with a ready smile for the customers."

"But the good start didn't last?"

"I'm afraid not. Tamsin seemed to lose interest rather, after that promising beginning. She also became, well, unreliable. I had to check everything she was doing. She gave people the wrong change a couple of times – not through dishonesty, but through genuine carelessness. But nothing does more harm with customers than that. And she forgot to put through a couple of orders."

"And have you any idea why this happened? She seemed from what you say to have made a good start."

Bert was thinking that this was the classic unreliability of the drug user who was becoming more dependent. But this innocent man hadn't considered that explanation. "No. I asked her once if she had some trauma within her family, or perhaps boyfriend trouble. But she just smiled and shook her head. Tamsin was always quite apologetic when she made a mistake, but her remorse didn't seem to improve her. She got worse, in fact. She became very unpunctual, particularly in the mornings, whereas she'd been an excellent timekeeper when she started."

"Could you give me some idea of the dates of all this?"

The earnest face wrinkled with concentration. "Well, she was all right for about three months, I think. Then she became gradually more and more erratic, over a period of about six months. Things came to a head when she was rude to a customer. I gave her a final warning. She didn't argue with me. She said she deserved it. She seemed quite upset, and for a moment I thought she was going to cry. Then she said I was quite right, and it would be better if she left there and then, without waiting to let me down again. She insisted on going that afternoon. She kept saying she was sorry."

Cedric Brown looked upset at the recollection, as if he still wished that things had turned out differently, as if he felt in some way responsible for the girl's death because he had dispensed with her services. Hook fancied he had been more patient with the girl than most would have been, had probably kept her on long after others would have sacked her. He said gently, "How much was she paid each week, Mr Brown? It's important that we know. I'll explain why in a moment."

Brown said apologetically, "Tamsin got a hundred and sixty pounds a week. It's not a lot, I know, but the business didn't really warrant even that."

Hook nodded. "She was a drug addict,

Mr Brown. That's probably why she became so unreliable. And why she behaved out of character like that with customers. What you've told me will help us to document the time when she passed from being just a user of drugs to being dependent upon them. It's also why I needed to know how much she was paid. There is no way she could have funded her accommodation and a hard-drug habit on what she was paid here. And for the last few months of her life, after you dispensed with her services, she had no regular income at all, as far as we know at this moment."

Brown was shocked. He said, "I was stupid not to have thought of this before. I've no experience of the drug culture, you see."

"I doubt if it would have made very much difference if you had realised what was going on. She was probably already dependent when you saw her work becoming more unreliable."

"Poor thing!" said Brown. It was more than a conventional cliché of regret: he was genuinely upset.

Bert Hook left the proprietor sitting miserably behind the counter of his cramped shop. He realised as he left that in the twenty minutes he had been there on a Saturday morning, there had been not a single customer.

Seven

It was on Saturday afternoon that the case got its first positive assistance from the public. A man appeared at Oldford Police Station and asked to see Superintendent Lambert, the officer he had heard was now in charge of the investigation into the Tamsin Rennie murder. Murder opens the doors which bureaucracy normally bolts shut; he was ushered straight through to the CID section and to the office where DS Hook was reporting to his chief.

He was no more than twenty-five, exuding a briskness and an assurance in this alien place which he could surely scarcely have felt. A salesman perhaps, projecting the confidence in himself which he hoped would extend to his product. A man whose attitude said, "Your time is valuable and so is mine; I won't waste more of either than I can avoid." He might have been an actor making an entry, thought Lambert wryly.

A moment later, he found that he was just that. The young man said with a nervous laugh, "Thomas Clarke. Tom to my friends.

Actor and dogsbody. Resting at the moment. Available for repertory, musicals and pantomime." He pitched the information into the room above their heads, as if he were projecting the words for a small, select audience. Only then did he look into the grey, observant eyes of the man who had risen to greet him, or take in the weather-beaten face of Bert Hook, or the crowded office, with its filing cabinets and papers strewn over the big wooden desk.

It was when Clarke sat down as requested that Lambert realised that this was the young man pictured in the dramatic profile pose against black velvet which Jack Johnson had brought from the dead girl's flat. It was an accurate likeness, but one so posed that it pictured an idea rather than a person. The photograph reminded Lambert of a seventy-year-old one of a young John Gielgud as Romeo. No doubt it was designed to suggest a similar histrionic potential to the agents and theatrical managers who might be persuaded to take on the young man's services.

Lambert studied him for a moment before he made any response to the man's declaration of his calling. Clarke wore jeans and a light blue roll-neck sweater. He had the slim limbs and coltish movements of youth, which made him seem taller than he was. His thin face was at once handsome and a little gauche: with a little make-up to emphasise his prominent nose and flaxen hair, he could have played a young Andrew Aguecheek as well as Romeo.

Tom Clarke had long, delicate fingers, as unlined as those of a marble sculpture, but they clasped and unclasped in his lap as he sat facing Lambert. This was a young man who did not find it easy to keep still. Lambert took note of that, and determined to play things slowly at the outset: nervous subjects were the ones who found it most difficult to hold things back.

Eventually he said calmly, "You asked to see the officer in charge of the investigation into the death of Tamsin Rennie. I am that officer; my name is Superintendent Lambert, and this is Detective Sergeant Hook. You had better begin by telling us about your relationship with Miss Rennie."

Tom Clarke threw his arms wide, then brought them back together and resolutely folded them. He looked as if he would like to get up and pace about the small room, but the set-up here plainly did not allow for that. "She was my girlfriend." He said it defiantly, as if he half-expected the claim to be denied. Lambert wondered what Tamsin Rennie's reaction to the statement would have been, had she been sitting in the room beside him. He sighed, studying the young face six feet away from him intently. It was the old problem with murder, the only crime where the victim was unable to volunteer any information. "I see. You're telling us that you were her only boyfriend?"

A flash of temper across that interesting young face was quickly controlled. "I mean I was the only man who mattered to her. We should have been married in due course, if...." The man who was so ready and eager to deliver the words of others was suddenly lost for words of his own.

It was Bert Hook who eventually said quietly, "If you had been able to persuade her to give up the others?"

Tom Clarke flashed a look of hatred at this stolid man who had spoken for the first time. But the weather-beaten features were so calm, so understanding, even sympathetic, that the outburst died in his throat. He waved the too-mobile hands for a moment, then said, "They were unimportant, the others. She'd already given them up. She saw the sense of what I was trying to do. If we'd just been given time, she'd—" Suddenly he sobbed, gasping for control, biting his lip and fighting for the breath which would not come evenly. He looked much younger than his years, like a grief-stricken child trying to be brave in public.

Lambert waited for a moment for the tears which did not come. Then he said calmly, "She'd have done what, Tom? Given up the lifestyle which was making her miserable? Married you, perhaps?"

Clarke nodded, grateful that these sombre men seemed to know so much. "Yes, just that. I wanted her to marry me, and she would have done, eventually."

Again Lambert had that fruitless wish to hear the reaction of the girl who would now never speak. "Eventually?"

"Well, yes. Tamsin had her problems, as you obviously know, but we'd have come through it, in the end. She was just beginning to believe I could help her when when—"

"When she was brutally murdered."

The sensitive face winced on the phrase, as though it had been struck a physical blow. "Yes. I came here to offer you whatever help I could, but it seems you already know more about her than I do." For a moment he was almost petulant with the thought.

"We actually know very little. Far less than you assume. For instance, we didn't even know of your existence, until a search of Tamsin's flat revealed this picture." Lambert showed him the rather old-fashioned posed portrait of his profile against the black velvet, and the mobile face broke into a surprising, rather embarrassed smile.

"It's a bit over the top, isn't it? I was imitating a picture of Ellen Terry I found in the library at RADA. Pure ham, I suppose. It seemed to impress Tamsin far more than any agent I sent it to."

"You were at the Royal Academy of Dramatic Art?"

"Oh, yes. Nothing but the best for Thomas, you know. At one time my accent would have been just right for RADA. Now they spend a good part of the time trying to knock a public school accent out of you. Regional accents are all the rage in the commercial theatre now, you know. I was allowed to be an effete public school Cassio last year, but only alongside a Brummie Othello being deceived by a Geordie Iago."

Lambert wasn't quite sure where this was leading, but for the moment he was content to find out all he could about this mercurial young man. After all, he had announced himself as a murder suspect at the moment he came into the room. "You were at public school?"

"At Shrewsbury, yes. As a day boy, though. We live about halfway between Hereford and Shrewsbury. So I escaped the routine adolescent fumblings in the dorm. Until I entered the theatre, of course!" It was obviously a line he had delivered before, and he looked for a reaction he did not get from the two large men who studied him so gravely and so continuously.

Hook merely said, "So you know the Shrewsbury area well, eh? That's where this Sacristan killer has been operating, of course."

Clarke looked at him sharply, but the Sergeant was making an entry in his notebook in his round, careful hand, with no trace of a smile on his rubicund features. It was Lambert who said suddenly, "How long had you known Tamsin Rennie, Mr Clarke?"

"A year, I suppose. Well, very nearly a year, anyway."

"And how long had you been sleeping with her?"

Colour rushed into the too-revealing features. "Now look here, I came here to help, and if all you can do—"

"Then answer my question! We need to know everything we can about this murdered girl and those around her." Lambert was suddenly impatient with the self-indulgence of this gilded creature, suddenly aware of the myriad pieces of information that were being documented outside this

93

room and awaiting his attention. "We need to know how serious your relationship with Tamsin Rennie was, how long it had been going on, and whether you think you were the only man seeing her. Then you can tell us when you last saw her and exactly what you know about her death."

For a moment, it looked as if Tom Clarke's fury would burst out in words. Then he controlled himself. Fastening on to the phrase which had most angered him, he said in a low, even voice, "There were other men. When I first knew Tamsin, there were other men. But that was over. I'd made her see that it must be. We were going to move away, to start afresh."

That old dream of the young, that you could move to a new area and cast off all the old baggage. That a couple were stronger than one, could give each other the strength to carry it through. It worked, occasionally. But never with an out-of-work actor and a penniless girl with a drug dependency. Lambert said, more gently now, "Where did Tamsin get money, Tom? She was spending far more than she earned, even when she had regular work."

"The rent for the flat, you mean?" He didn't mention the heroin he must have known about, his eyes flashing a question about how much they knew as he looked into his interrogator's face. "I don't really know how she afforded that." He looked at the carpet by his feet, hearing the hollowness of his own words as he spoke them. Eventually, he said, "Well, I do, I suppose. I just don't like to admit it. She was taking money from men, when I first knew her. But she gave up all—"

"She was taking money for sexual favours, you mean?"

"Yes. She was when I first knew her." He still couldn't bring himself to look at them. "It's against the law, isn't it?"

Lambert smiled. The man seemed suddenly very young and naive. "That's hardly going to concern us now, Tom. But you're saying that Tamsin helped to finance the rent for the flat by taking money from men who came there. It's important that you're completely frank with us. It has surely occurred to you that it could be one of these men who killed her."

"I've considered that. I'm sure it wasn't." Then, as if struck by the monstrous arrogance of stating this to a detective, he added apologetically, "They were a long time ago, you see, these other men. She'd given all that up, once we became an item." He produced the last phrase aggressively, as if challenging them to deny it. Lambert again wondered fruitlessly whether Tamsin

Rennie would have regarded Clarke and herself as "an item".

He produced the second photograph which had come from the dead girl's flat from his desk. It was all they had to offer, but Tom Clarke did not know that; he looked as if he wondered how much else they had gathered from the place, how many more embarrassing surprises lay in wait for him in the top drawer of this grizzled detective's desk. Lambert said gently, "This was another picture Tamsin had kept. It was found alongside the one of you which you have already seen. What can you tell us about this man?"

"I've never met him."

"That does not answer my question, does it?"

The slender arms were thrown wide for an instant, as if he meant to protest. Then he folded them carefully, like a child practising a new movement. "All right. He was an older man, who was visiting Tamsin regularly when I first knew her. She had stopped seeing him months ago, along with the others. He he was kind and gentle with Tamsin, from what she said. I expect that is why she kept his picture." He sounded as if even here it was important for him to explain that to himself. He said reluctantly, "That's all, is it? There weren't any other pictures of men, were there?"

Lambert wondered whether he should deny Clarke all knowledge of the sparse crop the SOCO team had harvested from that basement flat. Then he nodded and said, "Those were the only photographs we found there. Can you give us details of any other men who you know had visited her?"

He leaned forward, clasping his folded arms tight against his chest, giving at least the appearance of careful thought. "No. I told you, she'd given all that up. I didn't want to know about her past. I only know about that man because she had a bit of a soft spot for him. He was an older man in pursuit of a young girl who didn't want him. A bit sad, really. I certainly didn't feel threatened by him. His name is Milburn, by the way. Eric Milburn, I think. I don't know his address."

How easily the young dismiss people even one generation ahead of them nowadays, thought Lambert. Perhaps he under-estimates us as well, he thought. He said briskly, "Let's summarise what you are telling us, Mr Clarke. When you met her, Tamsin Rennie was supporting a residence and a lifestyle which she could otherwise not have afforded by an undefined amount of amateur prostitution." He held up his hand as the young man made to protest.

"As a result of a serious involvement with you, you believe she gave up the lucrative sale of her sexual favours. The employment and remuneration of young actors being as they are, presumably you were not able to provide her with replacement funds."

He paused for a moment, knowing that actors are rarely reluctant to talk about themselves, and Tom Clarke did not let him down. "No. I've been resting for about half of the time I knew her. I understudied three speaking parts at Stratford for the RSC last year, but I only got to carry the odd spear on stage."

Despite his intention to drop the Royal Shakespeare Company casually into the exchange, he spoke the initials with a hint of awe, as if he hoped for some sort of reaction. Lambert merely said, "Which leaves us with this unanswered question: how then did Tamsin Rennie replace the income which was no longer being gathered from her former clients?"

Clarke, diverted for a moment into his own life, had not been prepared for this. "I — I don't quite know. Perhaps she had saved a certain amount from — from what she had been doing before I met her. Perhaps her family had been helping her."

Lambert nodded at Hook, who said gently, "Come on, Tom. You don't believe either of those things. If you were as close to her as you claim, you must know that she wasn't getting any help from her family."

The thin shoulders shrugged hopelessly, the arms he had held resolutely folded broke free and flew uncontrolled and wide. "I don't know. Perhaps she was running up debt, for all I know. I thought I was going to get her out of the situation and make a fresh start."

Lambert said, "Do you know Tamsin's landlady, Mrs King?"

"No. I never met her. Never even saw her."

There was perhaps something significant in this resolute denial, but neither of them could see quite what it was. "She is not a lady who would allow someone like Tamsin to run up large arrears on her rent, I can assure you."

Again that hopeless, defeated air. "I can't help you about Tamsin's finances. We didn't talk about them much. We were concerned with bigger things than money. We were trying to sort out the whole of our lives."

The grandiose phrase was delivered defiantly, but the bravado was paper thin. Lambert looked at him for a moment, then said, "Indeed. And sorting out Tamsin Rennie's life involved even greater changes than you have indicated so far, didn't it, Mr Clarke?"

Tom felt himself shifting on his seat, even as he said, "I don't know what you mean. I've told you I didn't know about her finances, that we had—"

"But you knew about the heroin, didn't you? You must have done, unless your relationship was nothing like as close as you've claimed it was."

"I told you, we were going to get married. I loved Tamsin, and she loved me." With that simple, rather banal assertion, he was suddenly in tears. Neither of the older men opposite him moved forward to console him, to mitigate his grief. A man in extreme distress would reveal more than a man in control of his emotions, and long experience of CID interrogations had made them ruthless in pursuit of the information which was the currency of their trade. Eventually Tom Clarke gathered himself, volunteered them a look of extreme disgust, and said, "All right, I knew about the smack. She was going to give it up, with my help. That was to be part of our fresh start, when we moved away from here."

Lambert said drily, "I doubt whether that would have been possible, without professional help. Dependency – and according to the PM report, that's what we're speaking of in Tamsin's case – is not easily cast aside. But that's not our concern here. It's how

100

Tamsin financed the habit that has to interest us. On top of a flat she shouldn't have been able to afford, she was using heroin to the value of hundreds of pounds per week. Now where was the money for all this coming from?"

Clarke mopped away the tears from his handsome features, using a large handkerchief with a "T" embroidered in the corner, hating them for the question, hating them even more for making his misery so naked. "I don't know. I told you, my only concern was to get Tamsin out of all that. To make a fresh start together."

It was becoming a recurring chorus. Lambert said, "How long had she been dependent on heroin, Tom?"

He shook his head hopelessly. "I don't know. I've taken a little pot myself, in my time, and at first I thought that was all it was. But I soon realised it was much worse than that. She said she'd gone on to snow, and then to smack. I saw the needle marks, of course, as soon as — well, as soon as we were naked together. She wouldn't admit it, but I'm sure it got worse while I knew her. She needed more of the stuff, I mean, though she would never admit it. It's odd, but I never thought of her as dependent. I thought if I could just get her away from Hereford — She always talked as if she was going to give it up next week."

It was the self-delusion of all addicts: alcoholics, gamblers and junkies were all going to give it up next week. And of the three, it was the drug-dependents who usually died most quickly. Lambert said gently, "Did it not occur to you that drugs might be the source of her income as well as her trouble? People who are dependent lose all moral equilibrium. They will do anything to get the fix their body demands, when they reach that stage. Including selling drugs to other people."

"No!" The monosyllable came as a shout in the quiet room. Unless he was a very good actor indeed, this handsome, rather callow young man had never considered the possibility before. "I'm sure she wasn't. Tamsin despised herself for the habit. She'd never have started selling drugs to others."

He was desperate for reassurance, desperate to preserve the crumbling image of the girl he had set on his own pedestal. Lambert could offer him no comfort. "It's something we have to consider, until we find the source of her funds. I can assure you that once you are dependent on heroin, you will do anything to get the drug: the body simply demands it, needs it. Any idea of right and wrong is submerged beneath that need. That is what makes dependency such an awful thing."

Clarke nodded, accepting the logic for humanity, yet denying it for his own tiny corner of the human race. "I can see that. But I'm sure Tamsin wasn't selling on drugs to others. I'd have known if she was."

The lover's old illusion that the partner withheld nothing, that when you became what he had called "an item", two thought and reacted as one. Even in this moment of Tom Clarke's agony, Lambert found himself for a moment envying him his youth and its innocence. He said firmly, "Well, as I say, we shall need to find out how Tamsin was paying for the flat and the heroin habit. Whatever the source of her money, it may well have something to do with her death."

Clarke nodded wearily. "Well, you'll find she wasn't pushing drugs. Is there anything else?"

Lambert nodded at Hook, who said, "A few more things, for the record. When did you last see Tamsin Rennie?"

"Monday night. I stayed the night with her and left early on Tuesday morning. I was doing some painting and decorating for a friend of my mother's, in Shrewsbury, until this happened. I do it while I'm 'resting'. I'm actually quite proficient at it now." He grinned weakly, realising the implication that he wasn't finding much work as an actor.

"Did anyone call at the flat while you were there?"

"No."

"Any phone calls?"

"No."

"How often did you see Tamsin Rennie?"

"Three times a week. Mondays, Thursdays and either Saturday or Sunday."

"A very regular arrangement. Was that at Tamsin's insistence?"

Twenty minutes earlier he would have argued; now he was too spent for that. "Yes. She said we should test our relationship properly."

And thus left herself room for all kinds of other manoeuvres, they thought. "Had you considered living together?"

He seized eagerly on that. "Yes. I told you, we were going to. But Tamsin didn't want to do it here. It was going to be well, a—"

"A fresh start. I see." Hook wrote for a moment, then looked up into Clarke's anxious face. "Where were you on Wednesday night?

"When she was killed, you mean? You're asking me to tell you where I was at the time when Tamsin was killed?"

Hook was not to be shaken from his massive calm by the shriller tone in the young man's voice. "On Wednesday night, yes."

Tom Clarke looked from him to Lambert, as if seeking some relief or reassurance. There was none. Four experienced eyes studied him to check his reactions. He said in a low voice, "I was at home. I'd spent the day decorating and I was knackered. I tried to ring Tamsin at about eight o'clock, but there was no reply."

"And is there anyone who can confirm this for us?"

"No, I don't suppose there is. My mum was out for the whole of the evening. She goes to a yoga class, and then two or three of them go on for a drink afterwards."

Hook studied him, as if he expected some further elaboration, then made a final careful note.

It was Lambert who said, "You have a key to the basement flat, I imagine?"

"Yes. Tamsin had one cut for me. I should return it to the landlady, really, but I thought she might not take kindly to the thought of an extra key for the place. Tamsin said it was against her regulations."

"You had better leave the key with us. We'll see it gets back to her in due course. Tell me, have you been back to the flat since you heard of Tamsin's death?"

"No. Of course I haven't! Here, you're

105

thinking I might have killed her, aren't you? That there's things I might have wanted to pick up from there!" The coltish figure was on its feet in outrage, the unco-ordinated limbs moving wildly.

"Sit down, Mr Clarke!" Lambert spoke crisply, like a man giving a sharp blow to a hysteria victim, and the young man subsided like a broken doll on to his chair. "You had access to a murder victim, and the opportunity to kill her. So far as we are aware at this moment, you were the only person apart from Tamsin's landlady who had a key to her flat. We have to eliminate you as a suspect. The sooner we can do so the better, from our point of view as well as yours. Now concentrate, please. Tell me, would you say that Tamsin was a tidy person? Was her flat always clean and neat?"

Clarke looked puzzled. "She was as careful about the place as anyone else. The place was never dirty, not really." He sounded as if he was afraid of being disloyal, of a last, petty piece of betrayal.

Lambert smiled. "It sounds to me as if you're saying that she was like most other young people. Not particularly tidy, except on special occasions."

"Well, yes, I suppose so. Is it important?"

"It could be. I'll tell you why. Whenever

we have a suspicious death, our Scene of Crime team searches the victim's place of residence very thoroughly, as you'd expect. Now, they found very little of value in that basement flat. Everything was very neat, very tidy. The only photographs around were the two I have showed you. Every item of clothing was neatly folded and put away in a drawer or a wardrobe. I have to say that it would be most unusual for a drug-dependent occupant to leave the place in that condition. It rather looked as if some-one had been in there since Tamsin was killed, and Mrs King, the landlady, assures us that she hasn't been into the flat. If you didn't go there yourself, can you suggest anyone else who might have done?"

"No. I told you, I didn't know many people who knew Tamsin. She kept it that way, and I was happy with it. I didn't want to know, because I was going to take her away from it all."

They took his address and thanked him for coming forward. It had taken him thirty-six hours since the announcement of the identity of the murder victim to do it; they asked him why he had delayed. He said it had taken him time to compose him-self, to control his distress well enough to present himself. And he had really expected them to come to him, thinking they would have found lots of traces of him in Tamsin's flat. There had been several photographs of him there, he said plaintively.

He certainly looked thoroughly exhausted at the end of the interview. They dismissed him and sat in silence for a moment, each knowing the other and his methods too well to ask what he was thinking.

Hook said eventually, "I liked the lad, but he's a professional actor, so we have to allow for the fact that he might have been presenting a front."

"If he was, he'd had a day and more to decide on the image he wanted to project. Still, his distress seemed genuine enough. But that's the modern method of acting, they tell me. You look for the necessary traits of character within your own personality, presenting as much of yourself as you can, finding what you want for the part from within yourself, as far as possible."

"Proper Stanislavsky, aren't you?"

"You'd never have used words like that, Bert Hook, before you did that Open University degree. Adult education has a lot to answer for."

"Anyway, I'm not discounting the fact that our young man might well have found he was being two-timed by the mysterious Tamsin Rennie."

"Or even three-timed. Heroin addicts are

108

notoriously bad bets for relationships. I didn't tell him about the pregnancy, and he didn't appear to know about it himself. We may need a DNA test to establish whether it's his or not. I fancy young Tom Clarke would make a very jealous lover. And perhaps a violent one. All those modern notions about women not being property seem to disappear very quickly when beset by the green-eyed monster."

The two cynical old sweats of murder had their first serious suspect.

Eight

On Sunday morning, they had the formal post-mortem report. It ran to six pages, but it did not add much to what they already knew.

The girl was two months pregnant. She would certainly have known about her condition, which raised the question of why she hadn't communicated the information to Tom Clarke. Which raised in turn the possibility that someone other than he might have been the father. Clarke might of course have known and merely withheld the information. If so, why? And what else might he have withheld from them? For a man who had been planning to spend the rest of his life with Tamsin Rennie, he had known very little about the detail of her life. Or had claimed to know very little.

There was hypostasis of the blood in the shoulders, buttocks and calves, showing that the body had been lying flat on its back for many hours before discovery, confirming in effect that the corpse had been in the Lady Chapel of Hereford Cathedral overnight.

Death had been by strangulation, almost certainly by someone wearing gloves, but it was impossible to say whether the girl had been killed in the Lady Chapel itself or had been taken there shortly after death.

The stomach contents of the corpse indicated that a meal of fish and chips had been eaten approximately sixty to ninety minutes before death. That would tend to place the death some time during the evening, perhaps between seven and nine. That timing was supported by the evidence of heroin injection. There had been no intake for about ten hours before death – presumably the last injection had been early on the morning of the day of her death. Her degree of dependency would have necessitated a further shot in the evening, but she had presumably been killed before that fix.

There had been no heroin found in the flat. That left the question of where her next supply would have come from. But perhaps Tamsin Rennie had possessed ample quantities, which had disappeared from her rooms after she had been killed.

Lambert and his team were increasingly convinced that someone – whether the murderer or someone else entirely – had been through the flat and removed evidence before Jack Johnson and his SOC team reached it.

Tom Clarke walked by the Wye on that gloriously sunny Sunday morning. There had been no appreciable rain for over a fortnight, and the low river ran softly between banks lush with the green of high summer. It was still only nine o'clock and there were not many people about. He could see a family half a mile away, where the river curved out of sight to the left; he watched the father helping the smallest child over a steep rise in the path, heard the excited voices of the children calling through the still, clear air.

The very innocence of this rural scene seemed a rebuke to him, not the consolation he had hoped for. But there never was any escape from facts. Tamsin was dead, and he was walking alone here, wrestling with his guilt.

He greeted the family as they passed him, forcing a false cheerfulness into his voice, taking care not to catch the eyes of the parents. Then he walked faster, on round the curve of the river, watching a village church disgorge its congregation from beneath its square stone tower on the other side of the river. It was a scene which could hardly have changed much since Gray wrote his elegy, and Tom recited aloud a few of the verses he had committed so easily to memory as a child. The lines had simple rhythms, and the fine cadences beloved of an actor exploiting the range of his voice; they did not calm his racing mind.

He walked a long way in the attempt to exhaust himself: ten or eleven miles, without a stop, he reckoned, when he looked at his watch. But his spirit when he returned to his mother's old Fiesta was as restless as when he had started. He drove northwards slowly, hoping against hope that some solution would present itself to him before he got back to the familiar house. He wished for the first time in many months that the father who had left them ten years ago was there now for him to consult. But in his heart, he knew that this was a problem he would have confided to no one.

His mother was glad to have him home for Sunday lunch. She couldn't remember when they had last eaten a formal meal together at this hour. She knew he was only here now because that awful girl was dead, but she had enough sense to bite her tongue and say nothing about her. Tom had talked to the police yesterday afternoon; she knew that much. But he had said nothing about it, except for a sullen assurance in answer to her anxious query that it had been "all right".

He raised the matter obliquely when they had eaten their slices of beef and roast potatoes – in almost total silence, apart from a few half-hearted sallies from his mother and a desperate compliment on her Yorkshire pudding from Tom. "You were at your yoga class last Wednesday night," he said, as if he was giving her an order rather than asking her for information.

"Yes, as usual. And as usual, I went round to Jean's for a drink afterwards, before Amy dropped me off here."

"Yes. As you say, just as usual. Look, Mum, could you do me a favour? Could you just say you rang me here and spoke to me? If anyone asks you, I mean. They probably won't."

There was an interval which was probably no longer than ten seconds, though it seemed to Tom to stretch into minutes. Then his mother said, in a monotone which seemed to come from a long way away, "At what time did I make this phone call?"

He tried to be casual. "Oh, about eight o'clock, I expect. Any time around then. Well, perhaps earlier rather than later."

He smiled. His mother wondered if they taught you how to smile when it wasn't appropriate at acting school. She tried unsuccessfully to smile back at him.

Tom had never asked her to lie before.

"I'm afraid we are not in a position to release the body for burial yet, Mrs Rennie."

Lambert began with the formal apology, hoping he would not have to go on to the full reasons for the delay. If and when they eventually arrested the girl's killer and brought him to trial, the defence would be entitled to a second, independent post-mortem examination of the mortal remains of Tamsin Rennie, in case they wished to contest the findings of the Crown. Not being able to say farewell with the ritual of a funeral often added to the distress of close relatives who were already devastated by the sudden removal of a loved one.

Sarah Rennie did not seem to be fighting emotional distress. She nodded curtly. "There is no problem with that. The soul is gone. What remains is unimportant."

"You are very clear-sighted. Having a strong religious faith must be a consolation, at an awful time like this."

"It may be, for some. Superintendent Lambert, you need not treat me with kid gloves. I am not going to dissolve into tears in the face of your questions. I told you when I came to the police station at Old-ford, this death was not a shock to me, nor to my husband. 'As you sow, so shall you reap,' the Bible tells us. Tamsin had sown

115

the seeds of her death and her damnation when she left home and chose to live as she did." The lips in the long, oval face set into a thin line of satisfaction, the head nodded its affirmation, and the crow-black hair moved gently, as if in support of this irrefutable logic.

Lambert was nettled enough to respond. "You surely cannot believe that your daughter is damned, whatever you think of her actions. What about the grace of repentance? What about the infinite mercy of the Lord, who is surely the only one who could see right into her heart?"

For a moment, she looked as if she would like to engage him in theological argument, and he knew in that instant that she was one who could never be content with a faith that was merely personal, that she would be forever compelled to evangelise, to urge the logic of her beliefs on whoever would listen. She said, "Infinite mercy must always listen to the demands of infinite justice, Superintendent. The Book of Revelation tells us that we shall be judged by the tenets of scripture: 'And I saw the dead, great and small, stand before God: and the dead were judged out of those things which were written in the books, according to their works'. The note there is one of justice, not of mercy."

She looked past him, out of her square, sparsely furnished sitting room and down the long garden to the narrow border where phlox and roses straggled untended. A disturbed personality, this; one which at the moment seemed incapable of any generous thought. She had mentioned a husband, which set him wondering what any man could see in this formidable fortress of pride. Perhaps her bitterness was confined to the daughter she seemed so determined to reject, even in death. Or perhaps she was one of those zealots who found release in private in fierce sexual passion. Policemen over the years experience many personalities at the extremes of the continuum of the human temperament.

Lambert said stiffly, "We need to ask you certain questions about your daughter, Mrs Rennie."

"Of course. But I warn you, I shall be able to tell you very little. When Tamsin walked out of this house and rejected the Lord, she walked out of our lives."

"Your husband shared your views?"

"Shares, Superintendent, not shared. Tamsin's death does not affect the rock of our faith. I should perhaps tell you that he is not Tamsin's natural father, but her stepfather. Her natural father passed out of my life many years ago. I understand that he

117

died two years ago." She made it sound as if it were the natural conclusion to such perfidy.

"May I ask the name of the religion you follow?"

"We are Born Again Christians, proclaiming the message of the Good Book. We have formed our own group, without clergy or formal religious services. We meet to read the scriptures and reflect on their message."

In which charity does not figure prominently, reflected Lambert. He said, "It is a small group, no doubt."

If she detected irony, she was too disdainful to react to it. "Righteousness is not measured in numbers," she said contemptuously.

Lambert said, "I understand Tamsin left home about eighteen months ago. What age was she then?"

"She was twenty-one."

"And was the parting amicable?"

"It was not. We gave her the alternative: worship with us, live our kind of lifestyle, or live elsewhere. She chose to follow her own way. It was not the way of the Lord."

From what little they knew, that was certainly true. Lambert said, "How often have you seen your daughter since then, Mrs Rennie?"

"Only once. She came home to speak to

me, about six months after she had left. Apparently she had the opportunity of renting a flat of her own in that place where she was living. She came to ask for financial help. I wasn't able to offer it." The contempt was edging her voice again, an eerie contrast to the warmth of affection which surged into many mothers' voices when they spoke about their children.

"You didn't have the means to help her?"

"No, Superintendent Lambert, I chose not to. She could give me no guarantee that she was going to amend her lifestyle, to live once again in the ways of the Lord. I had no choice but to refuse her request."

"And did your husband agree with this decision?"

"He was not present at the meeting. When he heard the details of my conversation with my daughter, he fully supported me."

It would take a brave man to stand up to Sarah Rennie, Lambert reflected. He was already looking forward to seeing what kind of man this husband might be. Lambert studied her for a moment; the intensity in the deep brown, unblinking eyes, the certainty on the pale oval face as she spoke so dismissively of her dead daughter, were unique in his experience. For the first time, he began to entertain her seriously as a murder suspect.

He said, "You had your own reasons no doubt for refusing to give your daughter money. But did you not offer her any other help when you saw her in trouble?"

"She was not leading a life of which I approved. 'If thy right hand scandalise thee, cut it off '. Tamsin knew the beliefs we lived by. I warned her. She chose to ignore me. I cut her off." Again her lips set into that thin line of satisfaction at the staccato logic of her statements.

"I see. Do you know how your daughter was financing her lifestyle at the time of her death?"

"Should I?"

"Would it surprise you to know that we believe that at one point she was selling sexual favours to men to raise the money for her rent?"

The pale face twitched for the first time, but in anger at Lambert's boldness rather than in any spasm of pain for her daughter. "It would not surprise me, because that is what she said she would be reduced to if I did not help her. I told her I was not open to threats of that or any other kind. The door was still open for her to come home if she renounced the devil and all his ways."

And what a home, thought her interlocutors grimly. No wonder the daughter had not thought that an option. Lambert said,

"We have to consider it might be one of the men who visited your daughter for sex who killed her on Wednesday night. I presume you are anxious that we should arrest the person who killed Tamsin?"

He expected outrage from her that the question should even be asked. He was disappointed. She said calmly, "Of course he must be caught. 'Thou shalt not kill' is a vital part of our religion. I presume that it is central to any religion. We see many reforms as necessary in what passes for Christianity nowadays, but not to that commandment." No mention of her daughter: no passionate declaration that her killer must be brought to justice; instead, Sarah Rennie had moved away from the particular case that should have been vital to her to enunciate a general principle of justice.

"Then perhaps you can tell us anything you know about men who may have been seeing her."

"I know nothing. I wanted to know nothing. I told you, she had cut herself off from me by her conduct."

"I see. And did your husband take the same view?"

"He is a Born Again Christian, as I am. He lives his life by the same beliefs as I do. There was no room for compromise, for him as for me."

121

"I see. Well, we shall need to speak to him, in due course. We shall see then if he knows any more about your daughter's associates than you do."

He had hoped to rile her, to ruffle this icy calm, this unremitting dismissal of all emotions. But she said calmly, with that hint of contempt for the ways of the world back in her voice, "You must do what you have to do. Arthur will not be able to help you."

"That remains to be seen. It is surprising what people remember, in circumstances like these. Mrs Rennie, were you aware that your daughter was taking drugs?"

"I suspected it, when I saw her. She was already in danger of losing her job in the bookshop, and I knew from her eyes that she had been taking something. I am not so unversed in human behaviour as you might think, Superintendent Lambert. I was a nurse, until three years ago, when I determined to devote myself full-time to the service of the Lord."

Lambert only just managed to prevent a shudder at the thought of the tender loving care patients might have expected from this moral Boadicea. "I see. Have you any ideas, then, about the source of her supply?"

"No. I warned her about the forces of evil. I did not care to know the details of them – not that Tamsin would have volunteered

122

any information to me."

Or to anyone else we've spoken to so far, thought Lambert glumly, picturing the very different faces of Jane King and young Tom Clarke. "By the time of her death, Tamsin was an addict, dependent upon a regular supply of heroin. It is possible that her death is in some way connected with this. We need to find out whatever we can about how Tamsin obtained and paid for her supplies of heroin. It is too late to protect her, but there will be many other young people at risk."

"They make their own choice. They should know the difference between right and wrong and heed it. But I agree, the forces of evil should be opposed. I wish you luck in the war against them."

Lambert was irritated enough to say, "Is there no room for weakness in your creed? People make mistakes; humanity is venal. People, especially young people, need help."

"That is true enough. But if they are shown the paths of righteousness and choose not to follow them, there is no help that one can give. Arthur and I are the leaders of our little sect among the Born Again Christians. Tamsin's harlotry was an abomination in the face of the Lord, a disgrace to us as leaders. We had no alternative but to cut her off."

She spoke with real passion, and at last she had revealed emotion. It was her own pride in the image of herself that she had created which had been threatened by her daughter. Her anger stemmed from the damage the girl had threatened to the moral pinnacle her mother had built for herself.

Lambert said calmly, "Where were you on Wednesday night, Mrs Rennie?"

She stared back at him equally calmly. Her dark eyes registered the import of his question, but there was no fierce reaction to the idea that a mother should be asked to account for her own movements on the night of her daughter's death. "I was in this house, Superintendent Lambert."

"For the whole of the evening?"

"For the whole of the evening."

"And is there anyone else who can confirm this for us?"

Perhaps there was the slightest hesitation before she answered. If there was, her eyes did not flicker, nor her expression alter. "My husband was here with me. For the whole of the evening." There was the glimmer of an ironic smile on her repetition of the phrase.

But there was no passion: the only time she had revealed that was when she had spoken of her mission to spread the Word of the Lord, and of how her daughter had threatened that mission and her own place in it.

They wondered as they drove away from the stark modern house how far this clearly unbalanced woman would have gone in the defence of her image.

Nine

On Sunday evening, Sarah Rennie confronted her husband across the dinner table. "They'll ask you where you were on Wednesday night, you know, Arthur."

It was the first time they had spoken about her visit from the two senior CID men. He hadn't broached the subject himself: he was finding it increasingly difficult to talk to Sarah about her dead daughter. He said, trying to sound as if it hardly mattered to him, "That must be when Tamsin was killed. They asked you to account for yourself at that time, did they?"

"Yes. They asked me about how we came to cut Tamsin off so completely and I told them about her ungodliness. It seemed straightforward enough to me. I expect it was to them, once I had explained."

She was so sure of herself and her views that Arthur found it unnerving. He wished that she would occasionally show some sign of weakness or uncertainty in private. In the early days they had had conversations with each other, real exchanges of views and

126

emotions. Now, though she supported him unswervingly in their public work, they never did. It was usually women who complained when the only real displays of personal emotion were in bed. Now, he felt himself willing her to follow up her wild and unrestrained coupling of the previous night with some tender and intimate words of recall, so that he could feel there was more between them than the raw cries of her orgasms.

Unnerved as usual by her certainty, he said awkwardly, "You were very certain that Tamsin was acting in a wicked way. You don't think that might make the police think that you killed her, do you?"

"No. You and I saw how she was walking the ways prepared for her by Satan. I made the police see that too."

"Yes. Well, I expect you did. Your conviction is one of the things which helps us to convince others, Sarah." He put his hand on hers, pressed it gently, intertwined his fingers with hers. She gave him a quick smile, but he felt no answering pressure on his fingers. "So where did you tell them you were on Wednesday night?"

"I told them I was here, for the whole of the evening."

"And do you think they believed you?"

She looked at him, fond but slightly

puzzled. She hadn't really studied the policemen's reactions to her answers very closely. It was a habit of hers, now, which Arthur knew, but she was scarcely conscious of herself. She was so used to proclaiming the self-evident truths of the Way of the Lord that she scarcely looked for reactions in her hearers. "Oh, yes, I think they believed me. They asked if anyone could confirm it, and I said you were here with me, for the whole of the evening."

Arthur's heart sang within him. Sarah didn't seem to be troubled by untruths nowadays, once she was sure that the end warranted them. He hadn't even needed to persuade her, to point out the wisdom of standing together against the forces of evil and suspicion in an ungodly world. The lie was hers now, not his.

All he would need to do would be to repeat it, in due course.

John Lambert had told the dead girl's landlady, Jane King, how useful old ladies who spent their days observing the world from behind lace curtains could be to the police. At the time, he had not expected to find such a useful source of information in this case, but the diligent door-to-door enquiries by the uniformed police unearthed a watcher who was pure gold to the investigation.

This one, however, was male. As WDC Curtis, who was sent to interview him, became swiftly aware. Di Curtis was twenty-three, blonde, healthy, with a Junoesque figure, and well versed in the martial arts. Many a Saturday-night thug had underestimated Di's strength and skills, and paid the penalty. She was delighted with her transfer to CID three months ago and determined to make a success of it. Dispatched to the Georgian house in Rosamund Street almost opposite the one where the ill-fated Tamsin Rennie had lived, with instructions to glean all possible information from a source who was anxious to help them, Di scented a chance to make a name for herself. She would be patient and thorough, taking all the time necessary to add significantly to the so far distressingly sparse information accruing on the computer about the dead girl and her associates.

She had expected the man to be older. Somehow you automatically assumed that people in wheelchairs would be either seriously handicapped or seriously decrepit. This man didn't seem to be either, as he would shortly confirm. He ran his eyes appreciatively up and down her figure, approving the shapely calves, the skirt which revealed enough leg to stimulate his imagination, the slim waist, and the ample breasts beneath the light green sweater.

His head moved backwards and forwards as it reviewed his visitor's curves, tracing an invisible arabesque of her figure in the air of the spacious room. Only when he had surveyed her contours and approved them did he come back to her face and look into her wary blue eyes with a wide, unmistakably lascivious smile.

"Better than a sweaty sergeant with big boots!" he said. He appeared to think this an excellent opening gambit.

You learned to assess people's ages when you worked in the police. Di had found that difficult when she joined in her late teens, tending to put anyone between forty and seventy at around the same age, but she was better at it now. She put this man in his late thirties, reasonably attractive, well nourished and healthy of face, despite his wheelchair. She said, "It must be awkward for you. Being on the first floor, I mean."

"Oh, the wheelchair, you mean? That's not permanent, m'dear. Compound fracture of the fibula, you see. Healing up nicely, they say, but it takes time. Road accident. Passenger in a car driven by my wife. Well, ex-wife. Cow." He spoke the last

130

word without any real rancour, as if he was stating a fact, without sullying his credentials as a feminist. "It's only temporary, the wheelchair, and it's just the leg that's damaged. Everything else below the waist is in excellent working order, as they say!" He leered horribly. Di had a feeling that he was proud of his leer, for the simple but mistaken reason that he probably considered it an impish grin.

"I'm sure it is, Mr ?"

"Parker. Bert Parker. You can call me Bert." He thrust forth his hand, clasped her smaller white one between two strong paws, began a journey up her forearm with his fingers before it was forcibly withdrawn.

"Mr Parker," she said firmly. "Not one of the Nosey Parkers, I suppose?" The joke was out before she knew what she was saying, an attempt to mitigate the brusqueness with which she had removed her arm, and she instantly regretted her familiarity. For though with a name like his it could scarcely be the first time he had met such a sally, he cackled inordinately, enjoying the intimacy of humour, believing it must surely mean that this pneumatic vision fancied him.

"Very good, that. Very good indeed. Do sit down, Inspector."

"Detective Constable," she said firmly,

trying not to smile at this clumsy attempt at flattery. "DC Curtis. Here to take a statement from you." She opened her notebook and sat down on the upright chair five feet in front of him, then realised too late that it afforded him a splendid view of her knees and thighs from his position in the wheelchair. He slumped a little lower in his chair, smiling seraphically. She wondered if she should take him on at his own game, crossing her knees with a careless flash of white gusset, a vision which would surely be more than he could handle.

But she was not that kind of girl. Her mother had told her that she was not.

Di got up and walked over to the larger window of the two in the wall facing the street. This was a quiet bywater of Hereford, though not far from the Cathedral and the town centre. The window commanded an excellent view of the houses opposite and of the steps descending to the door of 17a Rosamund Street, the basement flat where Tamsin Rennie had lived. "I believe you saw certain things from this window which may prove to be of use to us in what is now a murder investigation, Mr Parker."

"I do hope so! I'd love to be of use to you, m'dear!"

The voice came unexpectedly from her

side; the wheelchair having arrived with surprising speed and silence. At the same moment, an arm encircled her hips, fingers stroked exploringly around the top of her thigh, where in Bert Parker's fevered imagination there would have been a suspender. A broken leg had clearly not dimmed his optimism.

Di Curtis slipped from the embracing arm as adroitly as it had encircled her. She had no fear; she was used to rejecting younger and more powerful advances than Nosey Parker's. But she did have a dilemma. This aging Lothario had committed no offence to bring her here: he was a private citizen, helping the police of his own accord. If she sent him into a fit of the sulks with a vigorous rebuff, he might refuse to help with the investigation. A refusal might not be public-spirited, but there would be nothing illegal about it.

They didn't tell you anything about this sort of problem on the training courses. And she dearly wanted to take back some useful information to the Murder Room. It was the first time she had been attached to the team of Superintendent John Lambert, a local CID legend who was held in appropriate awe by newly recruited DCs. She would have to retain the upper hand with Bert Parker – and as pleasantly as possible.

"How long have you been in your wheel-chair, Mr Parker?"

"Over three months, now. They had to reset the bugger, you see. Bloody boring it is, too, stuck in here all day with nothing to watch but the telly and the street outside."

"So you've seen most of what's been happening in the street during that time?"

"Most of it, yes. Well, nearly all of it, if I'm honest, during the daylight hours. I've been glad it's been summer, in that respect – bit more goes on during the evenings. And life's been a bit of a drag. Until now, that is!" He made a swift grab again on the last phrase, proving that his upper limbs at least were unimpaired by his lack of exercise, but this time she was ready and avoided him with a matador's agility and grace.

"As you know, we're particularly interested in any comings and goings from the basement flat at number seventeen."

"That's what the uniformed bloke told me. Said it might be important and the CID would be along. But I didn't expect anything as luscious as you, Sergeant Curtis." He tried his impish grin again; Di took the leer as a warning of further action and watched his hands with interest.

"It's Detective Constable Curtis, Mr Parker. Tell me first of all what you saw of the dead girl, Tamsin Rennie."

"Not a lot. Wouldn't have minded seeing a lot more. Bit of all right she was, though she always seemed to go out in tatty jeans. Bit pale and slender, too, for my taste, not pink and healthy like you. I prefer my girls—"

"Was there a regular pattern to her comings and goings?"

He stopped, disappointed, with his hands in the air. They had begun to sketch an outline of his ideal woman, so that they flapped a little, like pheasants that had been shot, before they dropped heavily back into his lap. "Not really. She seemed to go out most nights, but not at any regular time. Didn't see her much during the day. Saw other people coming to see her, though. Lucky buggers!"

"Tamsin Rennie wasn't so lucky, was she?" Di determined to cool his ardour with the formality of her questioning. "Now, it's important that you give me the fullest possible description of the people you saw going in and out of that basement flat, particularly any regular visitors. Do you think you can do that?"

"For you, m'dear, I can do anything." He made another swift grab, but she was ready for him now; she caught him by the wrist and returned the hand whence it had come. He sighed and said slowly, "There was a young lad. He was much the most frequent, recently. He stayed overnight, quite often." He brightened visibly. "Here, you don't fancy coming back here for a bit of overnight surveillance, do you? I've got a lovely big double—"

"Would this be the young man?" Di produced her copy of the picture of Tom Clarke and held it in front of him, taking care to keep just clear of those octopus arms.

Parker studied the young profile staring upwards so fixedly and said, "That's him all right! Poofy-looking young sod in that picture, isn't he? But I reckon he was giving her one on a regular basis!" His hopeful gaze travelled up the length of Di Curtis' long legs in her dark green skirt.

"How often did he visit the flat?"

"I should think twice, maybe three times a week. I'm allowing for the fact that I didn't see him every time, you see. But I did see him slinking out in the morning sometimes, looking tired but happy. Lucky young sod. And all the time I was stuck here, dying for someone like you to call." He moaned softly, then winked. It was a disturbing combination.

Di tried to be brisk and businesslike. "Right. That confirms what we have heard from other sources. Now, try to describe the other people you have seen visiting the flat, Mr Parker. Take your time, and remember this may be very important."

He sat back in the chair, savouring the idea of his importance with a satisfied smile. "There were a lot of blokes, when I first spotted them, a year or so ago. But I wasn't paying much attention, then, it was well before my accident. Here, do you think she was running her own knocking shop down there, this Tamsin?" His face was wracked with the pain of an opportunity missed.

"I really couldn't say, Mr Parker. Please concentrate on regular visitors you have seen and leave the speculation to us."

"All right, DC Curtis. Well, as I said, it's only in the last three months or so that I've been watching regularly. That lad who looks like a moonstruck calf in your picture was in and out all the time, as I said. But there were others, I'm sure." He screwed up his face and shut his eyes in concentration, then managed a swift tap on her left buttock as he said, "I've got it!"

You nearly did, thought Di as she moved swiftly out of range. She strove hard for an encouraging smile as she said, "You recall other visitors, Mr Parker?"

"Yes. Two of them. Not as regular as young fellow-me-lad, but more than once. Older than him, they were. More in control

137

of themselves, perhaps. More like me." He stared at her with a brazen smile, then winked again.

"Descriptions, please. As detailed as possible, but be sure not to add anything which might be merely imagined." Di tried her most stiff and official mode.

"Oh, I shan't let my imagination run riot. Except where you're concerned, m'dear. You'd be surprised what my imagination could dream up for you!"

This time he lunged with both hands, and his wheelchair shot abruptly towards her. But Di, feeling increasingly like an extra from a *Carry On* film, avoided him with a swift sidestep and thought that she should really have a matador's cloak for this clumsy bull. "Descriptions, please, Mr Parker!"

He grinned, then produced a drawing from beneath the cushion of his chair. It was obvious he had thought about this before she came, once the uniformed constable had told him that his sightings might be important. Di reached out, took it gingerly from him, and looked at it. She was half-expecting something obscene. She was pleasantly surprised. It was a remarkably detailed pencil drawing of a man of about forty-five, formally dressed in a suit and tie, his domed forehead accentuated by his receding hair. From the scale of the gatepost and iron railings Parker had pencilled in beside him, he seemed to be of average height, running a little towards a middle-aged pot belly. "You draw very well, Mr Parker," she said, glad of something safe on which to compliment him. "This is almost as good as a photograph."

Parker smiled, trying to look modest. "Draftsman, aren't I, when I'm working? Wanted to go to art school, when I was a lad, but my dad wouldn't let me. Plenty of time to draw now, with me leg in this pot, so I took my time over that. Glad of something to while the time away, I was." A delicious thought occurred to him. "Here, you wouldn't like me to draw you, m'dear, would you? I've always fancied I could do life drawing, and never had the—"

"No thanks, Mr Parker. I'm far too busy." She fumbled hastily in her folder and produced her copy of the second photograph the SOCO team had found in the flat across the street. "Would you say this is the man in your drawing?"

Parker set drawing and photograph side by side, one in each of his overactive hands. "I'd say there's no doubt of it, wouldn't you?" He tried to draw Di in to look at the pictures with her head beside his, but she had already made up her mind, and experience made her keep to a safe distance.

"I agree. How often did this man visit the flat?"

"With decreasing frequency, I'd say." He produced the phrase with ponderous certainty, as if he were already giving evidence in court. Again he had obviously thought it up before she came here.

There was no harm in a man giving due thought and consideration to what might be vital evidence, Di decided. "Could you say exactly what you mean by that, please?" she asked, feeling like one performing her part in a formal minuet.

"Well, he was one of the ones visiting before young Romeo came on the scene, I'm pretty sure – I'm talking about nine months to a year ago, long before my accident. Three months ago, he was still visiting – perhaps once a week or a little less. Then I thought he'd stopped altogether, but I've seen him going down the steps to the flat twice in the last two or three weeks."

"When was the last time?" Di had her notebook out now, making a careful record. Already she was imagining the gratitude of the CID hierarchy, could picture herself blushing modestly as she was singled out for recognition by Superintendent John Lambert, this detecting Titan she had never seen.

"He was there a couple of days before the

girl died. I think it was Sunday afternoon, but I'm not absolutely certain."

"And have you any idea at all who this man might be?"

"None at all. I think he might have been getting his end away with her, though. Before your young bloke took over, anyway."

"Did his visits ever coincide with the young man's?"

"No. Interesting, that, isn't it? I reckon you've got a fascinating job, as well as a beautiful body. I might even desire you for your brains, m'dear. Eventually. After a few years, like." He reached for her again, but this time a little half-heartedly, without any real hope of grasping her.

"You said you saw someone else going into the flat in the weeks before she died."

"Yes, I did. Older chap, again. Older than the one I've just given you."

Di's interest quickened. A new suspect, perhaps. All of her own, too; no one else had uncovered this one, as far as she knew. "Can you give me a full description please, Mr Parker?"

"I can do better than that, for you, m'dear!" Bert produced a second drawing with a flourish, emboldened by the reception his first one had received.

It was just as detailed, just as skilfully

sketched. Di felt that if she met this man in the supermarket, she would recognise him from the drawing. He looked about fifty, perhaps just a few years older than the man in Parker's first drawing. Unusually, but by no means uniquely in a man of his years, he had long hair, dropping almost to his shoulders; it was a style which seemed to accentuate his deep-set eyes and prominent Roman nose. He was not to Di's mind handsome, but certainly striking, which was often more useful from the police viewpoint. Strangely in such a depiction, he was carrying a briefcase, which looked in the otherwise informal picture rather like a stage prop. "Why the briefcase?" she asked.

Parker shrugged. "Because he always carried it, when he came there. Whether he visited during the day or the evening, he carried that briefcase. I thought it might help you to pin him down."

"It might indeed. Did he look like a professional man – say from one of the local offices or banks?"

"I'd doubt it, wouldn't you, with that hairstyle?"

"True. But he could own his own business."

"But I think I only saw him once in a suit. You'll see that I've sketched him in a roll-neck shirt and a sweater – that's how I remember him."

"Scruffy-looking, is he?"

"No, not at all. Smart casual, I suppose you'd call it. He didn't wear suits or jackets much, but he always looked clean and tidy. Bit like me, really." Bert pretended to inspect his immaculate nails, while watching through narrowed eyes for any chance to make a further assault on the CID defences.

While compiling her detailed notes, Di Curtis remained equally aware of her adversary. "How often did this second man visit the flat, Mr Parker?"

"Fairly frequently at first, scarcely at all in the last couple of months. I'd say probably only twice in the last eight weeks. I've thought hard and I can't pinpoint the time exactly for you, but the last time was probably in the week before the girl's death."

"Fine. Any other visitors you can remember?"

"No."

"And have you seen anyone entering that flat since Tamsin Rennie was killed on Wednesday night?"

"No. Well, not apart from your police people. The Scene of Crime team, do you call it? I could have missed someone else, of course, but I haven't seen anyone go in or come out."

Di closed her notebook, trying hard not to look satisfied with herself. She couldn't wait to get back and deliver her findings to DI Rushton at the Murder Room. She moved to the low-silled Georgian window, stooping for a last look down the steps to the basement flat across the street. "You've been most helpful, Mr Parker. If you should remember anything – Aaaargh!"

He had goosed her comprehensively at the last, when she had been so careful for so long.

He met her with a smile of seraphic innocence as she whirled in fury. "And you've been most helpful, too, DC Curtis. I'll certainly remember your visit!"

Ten

Lambert had the report of Bert Parker's observations on his desk when he arrived at eight thirty on Monday morning. At half-past nine, Arthur Rennie, stepfather of the dead girl, was interviewed. This took place by his own request at Oldford Police Station. Perhaps he did not wish to be questioned in the dominating presence of his inexorable wife Sarah.

The first thing Lambert and Hook noted about him was that he carried a briefcase. He came into Lambert's office and set it down beside his chair, resting it against his calf, like a traveller who fears to be parted from his personal bag.

He was a tall man in a dark brown suit, with the large lapels which were now out of fashion, and a broad silk tie which he tugged nervously as he settled himself to answer their questions. His hair was quite short; to Bert Hook's practised eye it was obvious that it had recently been cut. The sides and back of Rennie's neck were unnaturally white for the end of August;

Bert decided that they had almost certainly been protected by hair until very recently.

He was nervous, but that was not unusual for anyone who was being questioned in the course of a murder case. This man had some important omissions to explain away, some important questions to answer. Lambert saw no reason to make things easy for him. "It is now four days since Tamsin's body was discovered in Hereford Cathedral, Mr Rennie. Why did you not get in touch with us earlier?"

He was disconcerted by this head-on attack. He had somehow expected some opening preliminaries, designed to put him at his ease. "Well, I I rather expected that you would get in touch with me." In spite of his apparent discomfort, Rennie's voice was deep and resonant. An attractive voice – not one to forget in a hurry. "I'd nothing to tell you, you see. Well, nothing to add to what my wife had already told you."

Wrong already, thought Lambert with grim satisfaction. He would come back to that lie in a little while. He said, "Your wife took an extreme view of her daughter's conduct. Tamsin had offended her moral code, so she was to be cut off for ever. I would go so far as to say that I have never heard such a Draconian and unforgiving view ex-pressed by a mother in twenty years of

146

investigations. Are we to take it that you share your wife's views on her daughter's conduct?"

He shifted a little on his seat. "Sarah is very clear-sighted about these things. It can make her seem well, not very compassionate."

"That is certainly how she presented herself. What I am asking is whether you were equally without compassion, equally inflexible in your banishing of your stepdaughter from any family support."

Rennie cleared his throat. "I supported my wife. There is surely no shame in that."

"I am interested in neither shame nor the absence of it, Mr Rennie. Not at this point. I am trying to establish your attitude to and your relationship with a murder victim."

"Yes. I see that. Well, I supported my wife. We are both Born Again Christians, trying to bring the message of the Lord to the world and to re-establish the Christian values which have been so sadly neglected, even abandoned, in the last half-century or so."

It was Queen Victoria who complained that Gladstone always addressed her as though she was a public meeting, thought Lambert. That's how I feel now. For the man had mounted a metaphorical soapbox when he began to mouth his religious views, so that both he and Hook recognised that Rennie was delivering a well-worn formula. Sarah Rennie had said that they were the leaders of their own small sect; Lambert wondered what kind of disciples they recruited with this uncompromising message and attitude. He said drily, "You're telling me that you agreed that Tamsin should not be offered any help or comfort."

"That is correct. She could not be supported in her sin. If she had declared a full repentance and supported it by her actions, that might have been different."

The man is a whited sepulchre, thought Lambert. He knew he had no real evidence to support that view, but he felt it strongly. Rennie enunciated the same austere sentiments as his wife but, although smoothly delivered, they did not carry the same ringing conviction she conveyed. This was a man mouthing dogma as an escape from real thought: perhaps, indeed, as an escape from the truth. Lambert said abruptly, "Were you still in regular contact with Tamsin at the time of her death, Mr Rennie?"

"No. You wouldn't expect me to be, in view of what I've just said." The denial had come too quickly, right on the heels of the question. The subsequent explanation rang like an apology in the quiet room.

Let the arrogant bugger wade in deeper, thought Lambert. Let him spout his humbug until it submerges him. "So you didn't visit your stepdaughter in the flat in Rosamund Street where she lived?"

"No. I told you, I wasn't in contact with the girl. She wasn't my own daughter. She turned up at our house and appealed to my wife for funds to help her with her rent some months ago. Sarah refused, because of the sort of life the girl was living. I supported her in that decision. If Tamsin was refusing to walk in the ways of the Lord, there was no way in which she could be assisted."

"I see. How was Tamsin breaking the code you thought she should live by, Mr Rennie?"

"She was well, I believe she was living promiscuously. That is what Sarah said, and I believe her."

"I see. Her landlady tells us that Tamsin went on paying the rent of her basement flat, even after she had lost her modestly paid job in Brown's Bookshop. You say your wife refused her money. Have you any idea how she went on raising the money for the rent?"

"No. Not really."

"Not really? What does that mean?"

"Well, Sarah thought she might have been

149

selling her body to make money. As I didn't see her myself, I couldn't be certain. But if it's true, you can see why we couldn't support the little harlot!" There was real passion dancing in the last phrase, for the first time, and they could hear him breathing heavily in the pause which Lambert allowed to stretch after it. From a position where he had declared his ignorance of the girl's sexual activities, he seemed suddenly both certain about them and full of righteous anger.

Lambert thought with satisfaction that Rennie was getting in deeper all the time. "We now know for certain that your daughter was using hard drugs, Mr Rennie. By the time of her death, she was in fact dependent upon them. Did you know about this?"

"No. Though I have to say that it does not surprise me." His deep-set blue eyes widened as he addressed some point above the Superintendent's head. "Once the devil has tempted you to go astray, he will lead you ever further from the paths of the Lord, and ever further into the valleys of wickedness."

"Have you any idea how she financed this habit?"

"I have not. As I say, Sarah thought she might have been selling sexual favours. As I was not in touch with Tamsin myself, I cannot offer any further suggestions."

"And no doubt you have no idea what her possible sources of supply might have been?"

"As I have told you, I was not in touch with my stepdaughter. I did not know how deeply she had trodden into the lake of evil. How could I have known anything of this?"

He was a dubious modern man trying to speak like an Old Testament prophet. It was obviously a mode he had cultivated in the religious community he dominated. To the gullible people who shared his beliefs and were led by him, it might have been an impressive style, powerfully delivered. Lambert found it both hollow and infuriating. Without taking his eyes from the man's face, he reached into the top drawer of his desk, took out Bert Parker's sketch of the man with the briefcase, and pushed it across the desk to Rennie. He said harshly, "Do you recognise the man in that drawing?"

Arthur Rennie held the drawing briefly in his hand, then tossed it back on to the desk. "No. It's a long-haired man with a briefcase. I don't see the relevance." He affected a nonchalance which was betrayed by his suddenly paler face.

Bert Hook, ballpoint pen poised over his notebook, spoke for the first time since the man had come into Lambert's office. "Are you denying that that is a picture of you, Mr Rennie?" Hook looked as if he would like to record the lie, to make it official, so that it could be produced against Rennie in some future context.

Rennie must have felt the hostility in the room from these two old hands of interrogation. He picked up the drawing again, pretended to study it more intently, and said carefully, "I suppose it might be me. I did use to have my hair longer. Where did you get this?"

Lambert said, "It was drawn yesterday or the day before. From memory. I think it is a good likeness: the artist has skill, and he has observed you on several occasions."

"And then depicted me without my permission. Where did this anonymous artist get his sightings of me?" Rennie tried to force contempt into his voice, but his bearing was that of a man who knew the game was up.

"He is a man who is confined to his home, which is opposite the flat in Rosamund Street where your stepdaughter spent the last year of her life. He watched you visiting her there. Frequently, he says. He is quite clear about that. I'm told he would make an excellent witness in court, if it should come to it."

Rennie leaned forward, made a show of studying again the likeness he had thrown back on to Lambert's desk, without picking it up again. After giving himself time to think, he dropped his declamatory style and said, "All right. So this anonymous artist of yours saw me going into Tamsin's place. What of it?"

"What of it, Mr Rennie? Well, first of all, it means you've been telling us a pack of lies about your contacts with a murder victim. And secondly, it throws doubt on the veracity of any other statement you may choose to make to us. The most interesting thing for us, of course, is why you chose to lie to us."

"All right, all right! I wasn't proud of seeing her, was I? No man in my position could afford to admit to being in contact with a little whore who was taking drugs!"

"And what exactly *is* your position, Mr Rennie?"

"I'm the leader of a religious sect. You know that. A man to whom people look for leadership, in whom they have placed a certain trust." Despite his strong features, his striking blue eyes on each side of the prominent Roman nose, he looked shifty rather than trustworthy at that moment.

"We raise funds to further the work of the Lord! This is my business and the Lord's, not yours!"

"It may well become our business, Mr Rennie, if we find that you are refusing to cooperate with us. If you are a suspect in a murder inquiry, it will be our duty to investigate your financial situation." Lambert allowed a massive satisfaction in the thought of that duty to creep into his tone.

The Born Again Christian who had begun in Messianic vein now looked thoroughly shifty. "All right. I'll tell you why I was seeing Tamsin. But for God's sake, don't let it go any further!"

"You must know we can make no promises about that. If confidences are irrelevant to our investigation, we do our best to respect them. But there can be no guarantees. Nevertheless, I would advise you to be completely honest with us now."

"All right, spare me the cant! Tamsin was an attractive young woman. More so, I can assure you, before she became a junkie in the last few months. I am a man, fallible like other men. I have made mistakes."

And you now want the sort of compassion you were so ready to deny to others, thought Lambert. Any assertion that someone was an attractive young woman was a prologue to a sexual confession, in his experience. He said wearily, "So you slept with your stepdaughter. We meet it too often to be shocked. When?"

Rennie looked for a moment as if he would deny it. Then he said abjectly, "The first time? Before she left home."

So advances from her stepfather rather than the Puritan fervour of the Born Again sect had probably been the last straw which caused the girl to leave home, thought Lambert. But the reason scarcely mattered now. Unless this wretched parody of a religious zealot had killed her.

Lambert realised now that he would like his killer to be this stone-faced hypocrite who had been so willing to condemn others when he came into the room. He promptly checked himself. You had to remain objective, if you were not to overlook important facts. This man might be a phoney, might be milking well-meaning innocents of their cash, but there was nothing yet to make him a murderer. Lambert tried to keep the distaste out of his voice as he said, "And when she had set herself up with her own room, no doubt you visited her again for sex."

There was no resistance left in the man now. Probably he thought they knew much more than they did. "Yes. I even helped her a little with the rent, and I encouraged her to move into the basement flat when the opportunity arose. Mr Lambert, I'm not proud of what I did, but you should know

155

the circumstances. A man has weaknesses. Tamsin was a willing party to what we did. And my wife is—"

"Spare us the excuses, please!" Lambert had spoken louder than he meant to. He realised that his contempt for this despicable creature would come through if he did not control himself. With an effort, he went on more quietly, "We have established that you were visiting your stepdaughter to have sex with her, that you were paying her a certain amount of money for the pleasure this gave you. What went wrong with the arrangement?"

"I found there were other men coming to pay her for her services. She was no better than a common prostitute!"

"And you were the one who had introduced her to prostitution, by your own account. How sad a story that is! And how harmful to you it would have been, had that been revealed to your wife and your religious followers!"

He looked up at them sharply, taking the suggestion in their words, but not caring to challenge it. Again he probably thought they knew all about this, were merely waiting for him to confirm the details. The idea of police omniscience was a very useful one, which Lambert rarely chose to correct. Rennie nodded, licked his wide lips, and said, "She hinted in the last months that she would tell Sarah about it, if I did not give her money. I gave her what I could, to shut her up."

"How much?" To anyone with experience of blackmail, there was a weary inevitability about this.

"A few hundred, three times. Just over a thousand pounds in all."

"And when was the last time?"

"A few days before her death. I gave her four hundred pounds in cash. She promised me it would be her last demand."

"But you didn't believe that."

"No. I don't suppose I did, by then. She'd said she wouldn't ask for any more on each of the previous occasions. And she was on the heroin by then, an addict. Addicts are notoriously unreliable, aren't they?"

That was true enough. So was the fact that blackmailers almost always came back for more. Gathering money in this way was so easy that it made them greedy. And quite often provoked their victims to violence. Perhaps all three men in the room were aware of that.

It was Hook who asked, "When did you cease paying your stepdaughter for sex, Mr Rennie?"

He looked desperate at the blunt statement. "It wasn't quite like that, you know.

Or at least it didn't seem so, at the time. We made love, she told me afterwards she was in financial straits, I did what I could to help."

Hook, in the same even, patient tone, insisted, "You haven't answered my question."

Arthur Rennie sighed. The high evangelistic style of his earlier statements was now completely gone. "About three months ago. I stopped doing it when I found she was selling sex to other people. I said she was simply a prostitute; and she said I had taught her the trade. Apart from the times when I went there to give her money in the hope of keeping her quiet, I didn't see her after that."

It tallied, more or less, with what the watchful Bert Parker had told Di Curtis. Hook made a note of it, then said, "Where were you between six and ten last Wednesday night, Mr Rennie?"

"When Tamsin was killed, you mean?" Arthur Rennie tried a sardonic laugh, but what emerged was a strangled, mirthless sound. "I was at home with my wife, Sarah. With Tamsin's mother."

That was what Sarah Rennie had told them also. The old spouses' alliance, so familiar to the police, with each accounting for the other's whereabouts at the time of a crime. Whatever the CID scepticism about such stories, they were notoriously difficult to disprove.

But to Bert Hook's experienced mind, it left each of the pair without a reliable alibi.

They were a cheerful group, the five men who collected the refuse. The foreman never tired of telling the four younger lads how much easier and cleaner the job was now than in the old days, when you had to hump dustbins down the path on your shoulders and you dropped ashes and God knew what else down your neck if you didn't keep a perfect balance. His repetitions had become a joke with them, but they realised nevertheless that the job was cleaner and easier than it had ever been.

It was Monday, so you might not have expected any great merriment among the team. But by now it was also early on Monday afternoon, and this estate of new houses was the last job of the day: if they got on with things, they would be finished in forty minutes, with many hours of the bright day still before them. So the youngest man among them whistled as he carried the black plastic bags of rubbish away from the gates.

That was another good thing nowadays: most of the punters put the bags out for you at the edge of their properties. It might be because they feared you casing the joint for a break-in if you got round the back, as some of his more cynical older colleagues thought, but whatever the reason it saved you a lot of walking. And walking meant time, which meant you could finish your day well early if you got on with it. Damian caught the eye of a young housewife assessing the muscles beneath his T-shirt, whistled more loudly, and strutted his stuff with the bags. Racing hormones turn staid young men into optimists.

There were plenty of cars parked around these houses. They had garages, but fewer and fewer people used them for cars – they were too useful as storage places, especially if you had kids. Damien didn't notice the blue Astra which eased into the road behind him, nor the driver who watched his movements from a distance of fifty yards. Mind your own business was the code refuse disposal operatives lived by – unless the occasional totty showed interest, and you got twenty minutes when life stood still and everything else ran like a two-stroke.

The others knew the score; they covered for you, if it happened. And it did happen, sometimes, though not anything like as frequently as the lads back at the depot boasted it did.

Damian dropped the three bags he had just collected into the heap of fifteen on the corner and turned into the cul de sac of eight houses which ran off this quiet crescent. Bert, the foreman, had said there was a thirty-year-old housewife gagging for it down here, but Damian was still too young to be quite sure when his leg was being tugged. He glanced sideways at the front windows of each house, whistling his repetitive tune with desperate intensity to announce his presence, but saw no trace of the voluptuous nymphomaniac of his fantasies.

Behind him, the blue Astra eased forward silently. No one would have objected to a couple of extra dustbin bags – it would have been taken to be merely a householder being helpful. In the event, no one even saw the hand that quietly added two black plastic sacks to the pile on the corner.

Two minutes later, the Biffa lorry eased its way down the avenue. Damian emerged disappointed from the cul de sac, joined his colleagues, and vented his frustration by flinging the collection of bags on the corner with extra vigour into the savage steel jaws of the destroyer which churned to pulverise the rubbish at the back of the van.

From behind the screen of the Astra, keen eyes watched the items so carefully removed from the flat in Rosamund Street disappear into the destructive maw of this mechanical monster. The driver watched until those powerful steel blades removed for ever the evidence of who had killed Tamsin Rennie.

Then the Astra moved quietly forward and disappeared unnoticed in the direction whence it had arrived.

Eleven

Life goes on, even for policemen in the middle of a complex murder investigation. "Never forget you have a life outside the job," the young John Lambert's first CID mentor had told him, and twenty years later the mature Lambert passed on the same idea to his juniors. Christine would have reminded him that he was past forty before he seemed to realise it. It was his obsession with the taking of villains that had once almost split up a marriage most now thought rock solid. Nowadays he tried to practise in his own life what he preached for others, to look for the diversions of a life outside the job.

On Monday evening he engineered such a diversion from routine for Bert Hook, and his Sergeant soon decided that pursuing the murderer of Tamsin Rennie would have been much less onerous. They were playing in the Oldford Golf Club's knockout competition for the President's Prize: it was the last day for second-round matches and they had to play that evening or give the game to their opponents. Bert, who had never given a match away in a long and successful cricketing life, swiftly decided that in golf a walkover for the opposing pair would have been the better option.

Being new to golf, a game he had despised for many years, he had not appreciated that this was a foursomes competition. He and his chief had been given a bye in the first round, so the full horror of the situation had not been clear to Bert until now. With the air of one teaching multiplication to an eight-year-old, Lambert explained that each pair had only one ball, with which they hit alternate shots. "You drive at the odd holes and I'll take the evens. Just keep the ball on the fairway," said Lambert loftily, as if nothing in the world could be easier.

Bert found it exceedingly difficult. His nervous drive from the first tee bounced crazily into the cedars on the left. When Lambert had bent himself double and managed to chip the ball ten yards forward, Bert put it in the face of the greenside bunker. The hole was swiftly conceded to their opponents. "You'll soon get the hang of it," said Lambert. Bert felt that his tone lacked conviction, that his cheerfulness was already a little forced.

By the third hole Lambert, the man so

rarely ruffled at work, was saying through clenched teeth, "I expect you're a bit tense, Bert, this being your first game of foursomes. Try to relax." Bert tried hard. He tried so hard that he shot his long putt eight feet past the hole. Lambert gave him the sort of look he usually reserved for child molesters, studied the putt back with elaborate care, and then missed it. They were three down and their opponents were trying not to smile.

Hook actually produced a fine shot on a short hole, much to his own surprise, leaving a five-iron within five feet of the hole. Lambert holed the putt and became for a little while as sunny as the tranquil August evening. The little while extended to his own fine tee shot on the next hole, which deposited their ball in the very centre of the emerald fairway. It ended when Hook's nervous snatch at the second shot dragged the ball into the ditch on the left and his chief slid up to his ankles in mud in retrieving it.

Nerve is a strange thing, and it is tested in a different way in golf than in any other activity. Bert Hook, the man who had once walked forward and calmly disarmed a lunatic with a shotgun, who had been intrepid on a cricket field in bowling to Viv Richards and batting against Courtney

Walsh, found he did not have the nerve for this ridiculous game. The contest ended when he missed a putt of under two feet on the fifteenth and the opposition won four and three.

They shook hands with the victors and repaired briefly to the bar before getting back to the real world. The sun had set, but there remained the serene stillness and scarlet sky of a perfect summer evening as the losing pair separated in the car park. Lambert told Hook through clenched teeth that it was all useful experience, then forced a ghastly smile. Hook, regarded at work as an oddity because he so rarely swore, said it was a bastard bloody game and he didn't want anything more to do with it.

Golf, they say, is a wonderful game for cementing friendships.

The most dangerous task in modern British police work is undertaken by those who infiltrate the drug culture, in the attempt to discover and trap the faceless men who control it.

It is easy enough for the police to seize the users of drugs – so easy that opportunities for arrests are often passed by. It is only slightly more difficult to discover and take the lowest level of "pushers", those minor drug dealers who trade in drugs and are paid for it by those immediately above them in the ghastly hierarchy. Payment is often made to these people in the form of drugs themselves, for they have become dependent and are desperate for their supply. They are arrested frequently and fined or imprisoned, but only rarely are they willing or even able to reveal people further up the pyramid than themselves.

The difficulty for the police is that in this dark world of drugs, where the profits to be made are outstripped only by the human suffering caused, the junior ring of dealers know very little about where their supplies come from. They may know their immediate contact – though even that is sometimes kept secret and they merely know their pickup points – but they will not know any name beyond that, and if they know what is good for them they will not try to discover one.

For the whole of the grisly industry is infused with violence, with men whose trade it is to maim or to kill for money. Any challenge to the authority of the anonymous directors, even any undue curiosity about their identity, is met with swift and savage retribution. The drug culture is like a small, contained police state, whose weapons are fear and punishment. In many of Britain's major cities, up to four-fifths of murders outside the family are gangland killings, most of them with a connection with drug empires.

In the last decade, a small number of male and an even smaller number of female police officers have had the temerity and the bravery to infiltrate this criminal industry. Once they have committed themselves to the venture, they live in a strange half-world. They are beyond any immediate help from their police colleagues if they get into difficulties. Often, to convince those who supply drugs that they are genuine, they have to become users themselves, with the inevitable dulling of their senses and reactions. Yet the price of survival in this world is eternal vigilance. The apprehension about killing a police officer which still pervades the rest of the criminal fraternity does not apply in the world of drugs: the officer whose cover is blown is as likely as any other wretched tool to end up as a corpse in a canal.

One of the difficulties the infiltrators have is keeping contact with their fellow officers in the Drugs Squad. They need to report back anything they have found, so that it can be useful in this war against an anonymous enemy. Equally, they need to be apprised of any information about the world in which they move which other operations have discovered: at times, their very lives may depend upon knowledge of the latest development.

Yet the infiltrators have to be very careful about their contacts with the police forces they serve. Days, sometimes weeks, go past without them being able to make contact without endangering themselves. It is because of such danger that the Drugs Squad is a self-contained unit, pursuing its own war and jealously guarding its own procedures. Murder is such a serious crime that it can break down these barriers, but even a murder investigation has to proceed with care when it impinges upon the shadowy world of drugs.

The man who came to see Lambert under cover of darkness would certainly never have been taken for a police officer. He had a scruffy four-day growth of beard, a skin which looked as if it had not seen the light for weeks, and an odour which might most charitably be described as unwholesome. His jeans were shiny with dirt and split at the knee; his shirt looked as if it had been worn for at least a week. He sat in Christine Lambert's neat kitchen like a presence from an alien world – which, in a sense, he was.

They did not waste time on preliminaries, nor even on names. Lambert knew the young man was a Drugs Squad Sergeant and he knew that Lambert was a CID Superintendent, but neither bothered with the irrelevance of rank. Lambert said simply, "Tamsin Rennie. Can you help us?"

"The girl found dead in Hereford Cathedral? Not much. She's not on my patch and we don't have anyone in her circle of dealers. Hereford is not a prime target." He permitted himself a sour smile at the thought of the quiet cathedral city being a major vice centre. "What I can tell you is that she was dealing."

It was what Lambert had feared from the start. Feared because it pushed his investigation into this bleak world of drugs, where murder was casual and its instruments anonymous. But heroin was an expensive habit, and the earnings from Tamsin Rennie's sporadic prostitution were always unlikely to have supported both the habit and her considerable rent for the flat. "Do you know who her supplier was?"

"No. It's a fringe ring, lucrative for those involved, but too small and too remote from the centre to interest us. Too dangerous for us, too, from the very fact that it is small. It's difficult to hide a sleeper in a group where people know each other and their backgrounds."

"But you say it's on the fringe of something bigger."

"Yes. I know the ultimate controller, though we can't pin anything on him as yet. It's in the hope of assembling a case against him that I'm operating in Birmingham."

He hadn't given the man's name, even now. Caution had moved from an instinct to a habit in the world where he lived for seven days a week. Lambert thought he knew what was coming, but he had to say, "Give me the name of this top man. I promise we shan't do anything to compromise you."

The brown eyes in the young-old face studied the lined visage of the older man unashamedly, wondering how much this glibly delivered promise was worth. Then he said, "Keith Sugden. You won't hurt me if you go to see him. We've been after him for three years now, but he knows we're nowhere near him yet. If we get near, the bastard will disappear." For a moment, the hopelessness of his mission seemed to overwhelm him. Then he shook his head vigorously, as if to shuffle off his doubts. "I'll put out feelers about that girl's supplier, but I don't hold out much hope of learning anything quickly. Sugden's whole bloody empire is built on ignorance, with each unit knowing the minimum about those above and below it in the chain."

Before he could stop himself, Lambert

171

said, "Don't take any risks," and the sallow features creased immediately into a bitter smile at this ridiculous injunction. Lambert followed up gruffly, "That was stupid. I mean don't jeopardise the major operation you're involved in for the sake of this on the sidelines."

The young man nodded. "Murder isn't a sideline, I know. And I'd like you to get whoever killed that poor kid – I see too many in the same danger as she was. But I can't do much to help. The thing we're involved in could save hundreds of lives, in the long run." He sounded glad to iterate that, and Lambert guessed it was the sentiment he had to repeat silently to himself when he was alone in that world where he lived so perilously.

The man looked at the back door which led from the curtained kitchen into the garden, anxious to be away from this safe world whose bright fluorescent lighting seemed so threatening after the dimness of the places where he normally moved.

Lambert caught the glance and said, "Will you have a hot meal before you go? It won't take long to rustle up something—"

"No, thanks." A grin from the emaciated face, half of gratitude, half at the futile bourgeois politeness of this world he had forsaken. "I'll get what I need back at the squat." He bared his forearm briefly, showing the needle marks. "I dilute it, whenever I think I won't be observed. But you don't need much food, when you're on this."

In a moment, he was gone, roaring away on his small motorcycle from the comfortable modern bungalow into the darkness whence he had come. Lambert wondered whether he would go all the way back to the city on the bike, or whether he would be picked up in a layby by an unmarked car which would drop him within walking distance of his Birmingham squat. The Drugs Squad, operating in a world of savage and anonymous violence, used a caution that would have been appropriate in MI5.

He shivered involuntarily as he went back into the warm room where his wife was waiting. It was eleven o'clock on a Monday evening. The living gas fire flickered cheerfully in the grate. The colour television in the corner was replaying a prom concert. Christine was standing in the middle of the room and he went over instinctively and put his arms round her, holding the small body against him, wanting to reassure her that he was not threatened by the world she had glimpsed with his visitor.

"Has he gone?" she asked. She was shaken by how appalled she had been by the appearance of the young officer. She found herself at once resentful of him bringing the cold shaft of that darker world he inhabited into her home and guilty that she should feel that resentment of such a brave man.

"He's gone," John Lambert reassured her. "I said we'd make him something hot to eat, but he seemed anxious to be away. Perhaps he felt that if he sat in comfort and warmth for too long he wouldn't be able to go back."

He had grown used to resenting his lost youth, to bemoaning the way the years fled ever more swiftly. Now he was suddenly glad that he was not a young copper, starting out on life in the service.

Twelve

Lambert's first task on Tuesday morning was to ring the Superintendent in charge of the Drugs Squad. They had met, once, years earlier, but there was no time for polite preliminaries.

"I need to see Keith Sugden."

"I'd rather you didn't, John. He's a villain and a big one, as you probably know. But we aren't ready to move against him yet. We have to have a case the CPS will take on before we arrest him. At the moment, he'd laugh at us."

"Nevertheless, I need to see him. A murder victim was pushing drugs for him. We need to establish who was supplying her."

A pause. Murder, even here, even in the context of a Drugs Squad operation costing hundreds of thousands of pounds, could not be turned away. "It's difficult, John. We're getting nearer, amassing some valuable stuff on Sugden, but we're nowhere near ready to take him yet."

"Nevertheless, I need to see him. This

isn't the normal gangland killing, where we know we stand very little chance of arresting the killer. This was a girl who was only on the fringe of the drugs trade. I'm going to get the man who killed her."

His confidence impressed even the hardened man on the other end of the line, whose experience entitled him to be cynical. "I don't want the safety of any of my officers compromised. They're in enough danger as it is."

"I know that. I won't jeopardise anyone's safety. You're not the only ones who've been after Sugden for years, though it sounds as if you now have the best chance of putting him away. But he knows me. He knows I'm well aware he has a drugs empire, though he also knows I haven't the proof to do a damn thing about it. Nevertheless, once it was obvious that our murder victim was an addict, he wouldn't be surprised by a visit from me."

A sigh – the sound of reluctant acceptance of the inevitable. "All right. But for God's sake, tread carefully."

"I will. Don't worry about that."

For God's sake, mused Lambert. Whatever God you believed in, He or She had nothing to do with the hard drugs industry.

Bert "Nosey" Parker's drawings were even

more useful than he had anticipated. He was an artist manqué; perhaps, thought DI Chris Rushton as he collated information at his computer in the Murder Room, they should employ him to draw some life into those identikit pictures which so seldom produced any reliable identifications for the police.

They had already confirmed that the subject of the second drawing was Arthur Rennie, and used it to expose the tissue of lies with which he had attempted to distance himself from his dead stepdaughter. Now Parker's drawing of the first middle-aged man who had visited the dead girl prompted the memory of others. The dead girl's landlady, Jane King, so keen when Lambert questioned her to respect the privacy of her tenants, now recalled that she too had seen this man of about forty-five entering and leaving the flat on occasions. She couldn't remember when, but she thought his comings and goings had been surreptitious.

Once they knew who the man was, it became obvious why. It was a young mother of three at the end of Rosamund Street who provided the identification. It was a cause for raised eyebrows in the world at large as well as for the police. Or as journalist Joe Roper, who filed his copy for local rag and national dailies alike that night, put it, a matter of public interest.

For the man with the incipient pot belly and receding hair was one James Whittaker, local councillor, campaigner for the homeless, and favourite to become the ancient city's mayor in the forthcoming year.

Or rather, as Joe told his colleagues happily over his third pint, favourite until this juicy revelation.

In the wide valley of the Severn, four miles outside Worcester, an ivy-clad mansion lies hidden behind trees in a small estate of four acres. There has been a house here since medieval days, the first one being that of a fourteenth-century merchant who made a fortune from the wool trade and established himself here in well-serviced comfort, with a view of the river in front of him and the dramatic outline of the Malvern Hills to the south.

That house is long gone, apart from an ancient barn and a few stone stumps in the garden. The present walls of mellow Cotswold stone date only from the early nineteenth century, when a Birmingham toolmaker built himself a great business and retired to the grand house his standing demanded. At the end of the century, this man's grandson was much taken with

William Morris and the arts and crafts movement, and much of the original furniture, furnishings and even two wallpapers of that period survive in the high hall and the large, comfortable rooms. They are superior in quality and preservation to similar examples exhibited in houses owned by the National Trust and open to the public.

But no curious eyes are allowed to gaze on these treasures. The high gates at the end of the drive are manned day and night by a security guard, and no one gets past the entrance lodge without an appointment or the owner's permission via the internal phone system.

As the electronic gates swung back and he drove the old Vauxhall between them with Hook at his side, Lambert wondered how many people even in affluent Britain could afford to live in this high style and employ this many servants. Crime, he thought sourly, was the great growth industry of the new century.

And Keith Albert Sugden was one of the great successes of that industry. He greeted his police visitors with that air of ironic condescension which he judged would be most irritating to them. "We meet again, Mr Lambert, as they say in badly written thrillers," he said.

Sugden was a grammar-school boy who

prided himself on his learning. Brains were not rare in modern crime, but a decent education still was, except among fraudsters. Sugden found that it gave him respectability in the rarefied circles of society where his money now allowed him to move. He continued, like a man using the diction of an earlier age, "I can't think what strange notion it was which brought you here, and I won't go so far as to say that it is a pleasure to renew our acquaintance. But let us have afternoon tea and behave like civilised people."

There was no chance to refuse. The maid entered the room with the silver tea service on a trolley even as he spoke. Sugden poured the tea himself, handing them the finest Royal Worcester china and small homemade cakes with unhurried care, enjoying the ceremony of this very English piece of hospitality, enjoying even more putting the unwilling recipients of his hospitality at a disadvantage.

He took some pains to look as unlike the popular conception of a successful crime boss as possible. The guttural utterances of a Mafia Godfather were not for him. He was tall: though three inches shorter than John Lambert's six feet four, he matched Hook's height, and was immensely more poised. He was slim and graceful in his

Armani suit. His fifty-five-year-old face had a healthy tan which was set off by his carefully coiffured grey hair and the gold-rimmed half-moon glasses he wore for reading. He took these off, folded them deliberately with his manicured fingers, and set them upon the low table beside him. Looking like a man whose family had lived for generations in this elegant milieu, he said with a smile, "What is it that you mistakenly think I can help you with, Superintendent Lambert?"

"You can help us to determine who killed a young woman called Tamsin Rennie."

"The girl who was found in Hereford Cathedral? I applaud your murderer's sense of the dramatic in his choice of place, but I can't for the life of me see why you think I might be able to help you."

"You know perfectly well, Sugden. The girl was on heroin. She was drug-dependent and she had to finance the habit. I believe she was a pusher. A pusher for the drugs which were supplied by your network."

Sugden had scarcely ceased to smile since they had come into the room. Now he lifted his eyebrows. "*My* network, Mr Lambert? If I were more easily offended, I might make something of that."

"We both know I can't prove it, Sugden." Lambert was mindful of the need to protect

181

the Drugs Squad officers who were so patiently and courageously pursuing this man. He glanced round the sumptuously furnished room. "Equally, we both know that you're financing all this from the dirtiest trade in the world."

"We know nothing of the sort. If I were disposed to, I could make out a case for drugs. They bring much pleasure to people who would have barren lives without them. If you wish to condemn their abuse, you should know that in this country one person a month dies from ecstasy, one a day from heroin and cocaine, and one every fifteen minutes from alcoholism." Sugden beamed triumphantly as he produced the statistics, like one scoring a debating point in the senior common room of a university.

"And if you have anything to do with it, if empires like yours develop unchecked, those figures will alter drastically. You know as well as I do that our job is to enforce the law. We can't do much about alcohol and its effects, whatever the problems it causes us, but we can about you and your ilk. You're dealing in death, and making a fortune from it. And what death! You've seen how people die from drugs, as I have. There aren't many worse ways."

Lambert wondered, as he felt the anger pounding in his head, how he had allowed himself to be drawn into this. The relaxed comfort of this man's lifestyle, his easy panache in the face of a police visit, had got to him, as he had not intended that it would. Keith Sugden knew that too, and smiled his satisfaction in the thought. "I wouldn't agree, of course, any more than I would agree that I have the remotest connection with this trade. I don't think I can help you with the death of this girl, so there seems no point in prolonging our discussion."

He stood up, and Bert Hook almost followed him on to his feet, so powerful was the aura of this man in his own carefully contrived environment. Then, just in time, Bert realised that Lambert had not moved at all, and took his cue from his chief. Lambert said evenly, "Tamsin Rennie was a pusher for your drugs, Sugden. I believe she was going to cease doing that, to move out of the area, to enter a clinic in order to be cured of her addiction."

He had no idea whether this was true – it was a lot to build on the thin evidence of young Tom Clarke's vague assertion that he was going to take the girl away with him and start a new life elsewhere. But he had to get at Sugden somehow, and both he and the man opposite him knew the implications of what he said.

Sugden sat down again in the high-backed chair with the carved wooden arms. He kept his smile, but there was perhaps the first slight hint of disturbance in the increased frequency of his blinking. "You are no doubt entitled to your view. But what is it to me, who never even saw the wretched girl?"

"You know as well as I do that a rescued addict is a loose cannon. Especially one who has been a pusher. They're few and far between, but they're pure gold to us. They are the most valuable sources of information we can have about organisations like yours."

Sugden smiled, pursed his lips, nodded two or three times, pretending a professor's academic interest in a practical area from which he was far removed. "I can see that, I suppose. Reformed junkies might be prepared to talk to your Drugs Squad about what they know. Might even feel a missionary zeal to communicate their knowledge."

"This one was silenced before she ever got to that stage."

"No doubt she had other possible assailants as well as her drug contacts. They tell me that addicts exist on the fringes of society. They probably have a lot of dubious contacts. But I don't speak from first-hand knowledge, of course."

How right he was, thought Lambert. The

184

drug connection was only one possible source for Tamsin Rennie's killer, but he wasn't going to concede that to this man. "She could have been killed by someone you financed, of course. Someone like Fletcher."

This time he was sure he had shaken his man, however temporarily. Fletcher was a contract killer, selling his services to whoever would pay, but working almost exclusively for Sugden over the last two years.

Sugden said, "I should like to see you try to prove that, Lambert. You would end up with a lot of very expensive egg on your face." With an effort which was palpable, he forced his blandest smile. But he was used to playing this game: he recovered himself quickly, and so completely that within a minute Lambert could not even be sure that his opponent had been seriously ruffled.

He said doggedly, "She was dealing for you, Sugden. You may not even have known of her existence; it is even possible that you may not know who eliminated her, but by your rules she would have had to go. Your area manager would have known that."

Sugden's smile became more animated, relaxed itself into a grin. "I like that term: 'area manager'. You have a baroque imagination, Superintendent. That is unusual in

185

a policeman. It has enabled you to weave a detailed fantasy about my mythical criminal empire. You should set it down on paper some time, with diagrams. It might win a fiction prize."

Lambert stood up. He wanted to frighten Sugden a little, to let him know that there were cracks in the fissure of his fortress, that they were nearer to him than they had ever been, to see in him a little of the panic that could lead to rashness. From his own point of view, he would have dearly loved to press the man about the echelon of drug suppliers immediately above Tamsin Rennie in the hierarchy. But he had bluffed his way as far as he could go. He could not pursue the game further without compromising the position of the undercover Drugs Squad officers. He could not dismiss from his mind the vision of the haunted brown eyes in the young-old face of the officer who had risked his cover to come to his home on the previous night.

This time it was he who stood first. "We shall be back, Sugden," he said. "I don't know when, as yet. You think we're plodders, and in some respects we are, but we do have some old-fashioned virtues. Patience and industry, for a start. They help us to catch up with people like you, eventually."

"I'd say that was whistling in the dark, Mr

Lambert." Sugden allowed himself to turn the title and the name into a parting sneer as he ushered them out. "If, of course, I had anything to hide."

Lambert did not acknowledge the salute of the thug at the gate as they drove back into the sunny world outside. It had been a generally depressing expedition, as he acknowledged to Hook beside him. But he had seen enough to convince him that Sugden knew all about Tamsin Rennie's death, knew in all probability who had killed her. Whether the killer was from within Sugden's organisation, eliminating a possible source of danger, or whether this death was merely a convenient piece of luck for him, was still to be established.

Behind the ivy-clad walls of the mansion the Superintendent had just left, Keith Sugden had picked up the phone. He didn't think the CID were anywhere near him yet. But he was a careful man. It would be as well to warn certain people about the way Lambert's mind was working.

Thirteen

It was time, Lambert decided, to pay another visit to the house where Tamsin Rennie had spent the final months of her short life.

It was only four days since they had been here, but it was clear that the house was now undergoing something of a facelift. The handsome but scratched Georgian front door had been given a coat of deep blue paint; its brass fittings had been removed for the purpose, and cleaned and polished before they were refitted, because they now gleamed handsomely against their new blue background. The wheelchair and the battered, old-fashioned hatstand had disappeared from the hall, which was trim and neat, pleasantly scented with a bowl of pot-pourri which was set beside a vase of dahlias on the single low table.

Jane King was not pleased to see them. "I've said all I have to say," she told them as she stood four-square on the doorstep. It was only when Lambert suggested they could talk at the station if she thought that more suitable that she turned and led them through this immaculate hall to the comfortable ground-floor drawing room where they had talked on the previous Friday. "This is highly inconvenient," she grumbled as they sat down. "I've got the decorators in, as you may have noticed."

"I saw that you'd had the front door sanded and painted, that you'd got rid of the wheelchair and hatstand from the hall," said Lambert conversationally.

She thawed a little. "The wheelchair went at the weekend. It was only here because one of my tenants had a crippled aunt to stay for a couple of days. The hatstand is in my own flat upstairs. It's hardly necessary nowadays, but it belonged to my mother and I can't bring myself to part with it. The decorators are now working in the basement flat where Tamsin lived. You can probably hear them underneath us – there's an entrance from the house, of course, though the door is normally kept locked when anyone is in residence in the flat. I know Tamsin didn't die there, but I thought I'd have the whole place redone before I let it. You said you'd no objection, once your team had finished their work there, and your office gave us clearance to start the work." She shuffled some estate agents' brochures together on the table beside her, pushing them together into a plain cardboard file.

It seemed harsh, somehow, that while the girl's corpse lay still unreleased for burial in the controlled chill of the mortuary, all traces of her existence should be wiped from the place where she had lived. But that was a sentimental view: after all, the scene of crime team had bagged and removed anything remotely personal to the dead girl before the redecoration began. Anyone who was considering renting that basement flat would no doubt prefer that every trace of a murder victim's stay there was removed before they reoccupied the place. Lambert said, "You seem to have remembered rather more about the visitors to that basement flat since our visit on Friday, according to enquiries made by our uniformed men. That's why we're here now."

The chin of her square face lifted beneath the glitter of the bright blue eyes. For a moment, he was sure she was going to argue. Then she folded her arms across her dark green silk blouse in a movement of self control. She said calmly, "Ask away. If I can help you, I will."

"Very well. First of all, we have now confirmed that Tamsin Rennie was by the time of her death a heroin addict, drug-dependent, needing a shot of heroin approximately every twelve hours. She was not a registered addict obtaining supplies on prescription, so she must have needed considerable sums to pay for them. Our present belief is that she was a dealer, probably obtaining her own supplies free in return for the dangerous business of supplying drugs to other users. Have you any idea where she got those supplies?"

"No. I know nothing about drugs, and I'm shocked to know that one of my tenants was an addict. I'm pretty sure no one came here to supply her. Surely she'd be more likely to collect them away from here, nearer to the places where she dealt in them?"

She was deadly serious now, seemingly disturbed by the notion that her house could have been used even on the periphery of this trade. And what she suggested was true enough: the dead girl's contacts were more likely to have been in or around the sleazy pubs and clubs where she dealt than in this quiet Georgian street. At least the suggestion that drugs might have changed hands here seemed to have shaken Jane King a little, so that she might now be more forthcoming about other things. Lambert said, "We need to know much more about the men who were in contact with Tamsin

191

in the months before her death. Did you know that Tamsin's stepfather visited her regularly, at least in the early days of her stay here?"

"No." She stared him steadily in the face, refusing to enlarge on her answer.

Lambert produced a photocopy of Parker's drawing. "This is Arthur Rennie. Are you sure you haven't seen him before?"

She looked, then held the picture before her for a moment. Whether she was studying it and cudgelling her memory or calculating how to phrase her answer, he could not be sure. When her reply came, it had a forced formality, as if caution was dictating she gave the bare facts, lest she implicate Rennie. "I have seen him, yes. I remember him visiting Tamsin, when she first came to stay here. But I did not know his identity, not until now. It was not my business to know it. I told you on Friday: my residents are entitled to their privacy. That is one of the reasons why they pay me rent."

"Of course. But you didn't know about this man's relationship with the dead girl?"

"No. Now that you've prodded my memory, I seem to remember seeing him here more than once. He might even have come after she'd transferred to the basement flat, but I wouldn't be sure of that."

"Now that you've remembered him, let

me push you a little further. Can you recall what sort of relationship Tamsin might have had with him?"

The blue eyes narrowed a little, studying him coolly, wondering quite what he was about, where this might be leading. She crossed her legs, while the CID men noted automatically the quality of her light brown linen trousers. She was older than they had thought on their first visit, Bert Hook decided as she glanced at him, probably in her mid-forties, well preserved, expensively clad and discreetly made up. She was an attractive woman, but there was a quality of hardness about her which made one pause. Hook, with his upbringing in Barnardo's homes, was an expert on middle-class ladies of smart appearance and iron will.

Now she said, "I didn't see enough of the man to form any estimation of his relationship with Tamsin. But I can tell you a little, because she talked to me once or twice when she was paying her rent. I know she didn't get on with her mother. And I gather there had been well, an incident with her stepfather. She said he had assaulted her. I gathered that was one reason why she had left home and taken a room here in the first place. I only have Tamsin's word for that, of course. It may not even be true. I wouldn't like to cause trouble for anyone. I'm only telling you now because she's been murdered."

"As she had been at the time of our last visit, Mrs King," said Lambert drily. "It would have been helpful to have this information then." He found the landlady's cool composure irritating. But at least she seemed to be more cooperative now; for a woman who had begun this meeting by stating that she had said all she had to say, she was now providing a lot of information. Perhaps she was frightened, as many were, by the mention of drugs, by the need to reject the notion that her house had been the place where they changed hands.

Whatever the reason, they must capitalise upon this willingness to deliver information. "Perhaps we can now stir your memory about other things: I also asked you on Friday if you had any idea how she was raising the extra money to pay for that basement flat, but you were unable to help us. You said, if I remember right, that she mostly paid in cash, but you didn't know where it came from."

She nodded slowly, ignoring the slur on her honesty at their first meeting, too shrewd to be drawn into a defence of her behaviour four days earlier. Lambert was forced to make his own running. "We now have reason to believe that Tamsin Rennie was entertaining men for money, was selling her body to sustain the lifestyle she had taken on. Are you saying that you were completely unaware of these activities?"

She took her time, refusing to descend into the anger that might have been revealing. "That had not struck me as a possibility at the time. Now that you mention it, I can see that it is a possibility. The acts would support it: she had a number of male visitors, more than you might expect a girl of her background to entertain, I suppose. I expect I'm rather naive in these matters."

She looked so far from naive that Lambert found an involuntary smile on his lips. "You're saying you had no idea of this activity at the time?"

"If I'd thought she was using my flat for the purposes of prostitution, which I presume is what you are saying, she'd have been on her way very quickly."

"I see." For a moment, Lambert wondered whether this smartly dressed, worldly wise woman had been acting as pimp, furnishing clients for Tamsin Rennie. It hardly seemed likely. If she was the madam of a disorderly house behind the staid exterior of 17 Rosamund Street, she would certainly have been acting for several girls, and enquiries among her tenants had revealed no other women making their living in that way. He said, "Well, now that you are belatedly aware of these activities, can you recall in a little more detail any others among her clients? I need hardly tell you that in a murder investigation we must follow up any such contacts until they are eliminated from the inquiry."

She refused still to be insulted by his tone, which told her more plainly than words that he believed she had withheld information on his last visit here. She looked past the two large men for a moment to the clump of salvias which blazed so brightly in the enclosed quiet of the garden beyond the window; she seemed to be reviewing the last months and trying to picture the men who had come to see her basement tenant.

Eventually she said, "I was aware that there were men, but as I didn't know what you are now telling me was going on, I didn't pay a lot of attention. My tenants, as I have repeatedly explained to you, are entitled to their privacy."

"But you must have been aware, for instance, of Tom Clarke, the young man who wanted to marry Tamsin Rennie."

She shrugged. "Is that his name? The lad who wants to be an actor? I didn't pay much attention to him. You expect girls of Tamsin's age to have a regular boyfriend."

196

"Yet you know how this one earns his living, it seems."

She smiled at him, refusing to take offence. "I expect Tamsin told me. We chatted a little, when we happened to meet. But that wasn't often, once she had taken the flat in the basement with its own entrance. It was mostly when she came up to pay her rent."

"Did she ever mention any violence from him? Or suggest he was becoming a nuisance?"

"No. Not to me. For what it's worth, I got the impression that she was rather fond of him, and becoming more so. I should emphasise that it's just that: an impression. I can't recall Tamsin actually saying that, and I've never spoken to the boy himself. Is he now a suspect?"

Lambert smiled. It was the first naive question she had asked, and they both recognised it immediately as that. "The boyfriend always has to be eliminated in cases like this. Just as the husband has to be. And at a further remove, in the next circle moving outwards from the centre, anyone who lived in close proximity to the victim and thus had the opportunity. That is why members of my team have questioned all your tenants in the last few days."

"And why the man in charge of the case

197

has come here twice to speak to the victim's landlady?"

They smiled at each other, each appreciating the swiftness of the mind behind the face. Then Lambert said, "There is a discrepancy in our records. Your friends the Frasers say you arrived for dinner with them last Wednesday at some time after eight. You told us it was at twenty past seven."

She smiled. "If Don Fraser says it was later, I'm sure he's right. He's a very precise man, Don. I think I said at the time that I wasn't sure about the time, that I didn't expect to be quizzed about it by the CID."

Lambert nodded. "You did indeed. There was another reason for this second visit. Sergeant Hook and I also suspected that you would be able to help us with information about the victim and her associates. As you are now most usefully doing."

"Well, I didn't see much of the boyfriend, though I was aware he was visiting regularly, was sometimes staying overnight."

"What about Tamsin's other visitors?"

She breathed in, revealing nothing of what she was about to say in the quiet, square face within the neat framing of short dark hair. She looked out through the window at her garden and said, "There was one man I did recognise. Councillor Whittaker."

She looked back from the flower border to Lambert's face on her last words, as if curious to see whether the name would emerge as the bombshell it might have been.

It was his turn to be deadpan. "How often did you see him here?"

"Several times. I cannot be precise. But I did see him going into Tamsin's flat about ten days ago." As she watched Hook recording her words, she had a slight, rueful smile. Perhaps she was considering the local impact of this when it reached the press, as it surely must.

"And you think he had visited her upon a regular basis?"

"I did not say regular. I said he had been several times: that is rather different."

Lambert smiled, admiring her precision in spite of himself. "Yet you remember Councillor Whittaker's last visit – if indeed it was his last one – pretty clearly. Ten days ago, you said."

"I remember it because there is something to pinpoint it in my mind, Superintendent Lambert, that is all. The flat is below this room: you have heard the men at work down there yourselves this afternoon. It was a warm evening; the windows were open downstairs then as they are now. So was the window in this room." She walked over and lifted the bottom of the sash window; they heard the noise of the workmen's radio from the flat below quite clearly. "I heard the sound of an argument. A heated argument, in fact. He was arguing that Tamsin should leave the flat. What you have told me this afternoon gives a little more sense to it. I only caught the odd phrase, but I now think James Whittaker was trying to get Tamsin to go away and set up home with him."

"And yet you withheld all of this from us four days ago. You can hardly have thought it insignificant."

"I mind my own business. It is much the best way to conduct affairs, if you are a landlady, I can assure you. My reaction at the time was to shut the window and get on with my own life. I heard the sound of raised voices and thought it was private."

"But you now think that Councillor Whittaker was one of Tamsin Rennie's sexual clients. That this was perhaps a lover's quarrel."

"That is for you to follow up, not me, Superintendent. But since you seem to think I have been less than forthcoming and now ask me to speculate, I will do so. In the light of what you have told me today, I think that James Whittaker had been paying for sexual favours over some months; that he had become besotted with a pretty young girl twenty years younger than him, that he wished to reform her ways and make her his permanent partner. I believe that that was what the row I heard was all about."

It was a major switch from withholding information to speculating as far as this. Lambert noted the change of heart, had even time to wonder quite what had prompted it, but did not comment upon it; what Jane King was now saying was far too interesting for that. He said with a smile, "How far is this conjecture and how far fact, Mrs King?"

She looked at him shrewdly, her head a little on one side, as if estimating an opponent. "It is conjecture based on the few facts I know, that is all. My theory fits in with the very limited fragments I saw of the dealings between Tamsin and James Whittaker. I know a little about Mr Whittaker because he happens to be my local councillor. He is a widower with no children who lives on his own in quite a large house within half a mile of here. Just on the other side of the Cathedral, as a matter of fact."

She paused for the implications of her last phrase to be digested by all of them, including perhaps herself. None of them smiled at the mention of the Cathedral: this was now too serious for that. Lambert merely said, "You think Mr Whittaker is a lonely man?"

Jane King shook her head, coolly estimating how far she should go with this. "I can't say that: I don't know him well enough. It would fit the facts, in so far as I know them. Councillor Whittaker visits a nubile girl, over twenty years younger than him, for what now appears to be sexual purposes. He becomes besotted with her, asks her to live with him in his own house perhaps to marry him, for all we know, and—"

"You're saying that a man wise in the ways of the world, with aspirations to become mayor of his city, asks a girl who is little better than a streetwalker to become his permanent partner?"

Even as he said it, Lambert knew that it wasn't as preposterous as he made it sound. And as if she read his mind, Jane King said with a sour smile, "Men always think they can reform fallen girls."

Lambert wondered what worlds of experience lay behind her quiet contempt for his gender. He said, "Is that what the argument between the two of them was about? The one you just said you heard a few days before Tamsin was killed?"

She nodded. "I only heard snatches, you

understand. But he was certainly arguing that she should go somewhere with him. I thought at the time that it might be on some trip or other, a temporary arrangement. Now, in view of the other facts you have filled in for me, I'm inclined to think he was suggesting a more permanent liaison. I don't think my view would stand up in the face of a hostile cross-examination in court, mind. A clever lawyer would tear me apart, because I didn't hear enough to be certain. I'm just giving you my thoughts because you asked for them."

And you think that Whittaker might have killed the girl in a fit of jealous rage a few days later, thought Lambert. But you are too clever to state anything so unpleasant, Jane King. Leave it to the CID to do the dirty work. Well, fair enough. She had been far more forthcoming about the men who had known Tamsin Rennie on this visit than on their first one. Whatever the reasons for that, she had confirmed for them that both Tom Clarke and James Whittaker should be added to the mother and stepfather of the dead girl as serious murder suspects.

What she had not been able to help them with was any clue to the threat which might have come from the dark world of drugs which lay beyond the facts they had now assembled about this death.

Fourteen

At seven twenty on the morning of Wednesday, August 24th, Christine Lambert found her husband smelling the roses, the policeman's traditional escape from reality.

It was a glorious morning, with the garden burgeoning in high summer profusion. "You've done a grand job on those weeds whilst I've been busy," said John. In the complex double-speak of marriage, this was an acknowledgement that she was in full health again after the heart bypass operation she had undergone a few months earlier.

They toured the garden, remarking the unique beauty of the hybrid tea blooms, congratulating themselves on the way the new clematis was cloaking the old apple tree with its cerise flowers, talking nonsense to their tame thrush, which hopped along four yards behind them. It was a sane, ordered world, which helped to set the sometimes crazy one outside into a proper perspective.

Lambert had thought to enjoy a few

moments alone here, but he was glad now to find Christine at his side. They did not touch each other as they walked around the dew-soft lawns, but each knew that this was a moment of intimacy, a reassertion of their personal world and its values. It was a world that had been threatened twice in the last two years, first by cancer and a mastectomy for Christine, and more lately by her heart bypass operation. They were unwelcome reminders of mortality, but they had brought the pair closer than ever before in a relationship which had been strengthened by the vicissitudes of its early years.

Christine knew better than to bring anything external into their admiration of the early morning garden. It was not until he was finishing his toast that she asked him about the progress of his investigation into what the papers were now headlining as "Murder in the Cathedral".

"It will be a week ago tonight that she died," he said. "A week tomorrow morning since the body was discovered."

She knew what he meant without needing an explanation. Most murders are solved within the first week. A high proportion of those unsolved at the end of that time are never solved. Although the official line is that cases never close until an arrest is made and an offender is charged, there comes at some stage a gradual withdrawal of resources, a diversion of personnel to other, more urgent and hopefully more rewarding fields.

"How's it going, then?" she asked as she poured the massive beaker of tea with which he always concluded his breakfast. At one time she would never have asked. He would have hugged the details to himself like a priest guarding a confession, and she would have scorned to show any interest in the work which seemed like a black hole between them. Now she was genuinely interested in whatever crumbs he chose to volunteer to her.

"It's difficult to say. We do know a lot more about the dead girl than we knew six days ago, but I'm still not sure which are the relevant bits. It's taken more time than I'd have wanted to get this far; there's one man who seems to be a strong suspect whom I haven't even seen yet."

He didn't volunteer that it was a local councillor, and she had more sense than to ask him for details. She put her hands on the back of his neck as he sat at the table, massaging it on the left-hand side, where she knew it was always stiff. "If I know Superintendent Lambert, he'll produce something out of the hat in the next few days. The Chief Constable more or less said that on Central Television news last night."

"Did he really? Well, I'm glad he's so confident!" But there was no resentment in his irony; he was glad enough for the CC or anyone else to give statements to the media and keep them off his back.

Christine went to shut the garage doors as he reversed with some difficulty down the curving drive. She was going to get him an electronic garage-door opener for his birthday. She knew he would veto it if it were announced beforehand, but find it thoroughly convenient after a week's use. Silly old sod, she thought affectionately.

He thought he might have shut up about the case too abruptly within the bungalow, as had always been his wont, so he threw her a last few words through the open window of the car. "I've got a nasty feeling that girl's death is going to be drug related," he said gloomily.

She knew what that meant. He was fearful they might never find who had committed the newspapers' Murder in the Cathedral.

The first thing which struck Lambert and Hook about James Whittaker, Councillor and prospective mayor of Hereford, was how remarkable a likeness of him Bert "Nosey" Parker had managed to capture in a pencilled sketch.

Whittaker was of average height or a little less. He had a high forehead above large brown eyes and a nose which looked curiously malleable, as if a child could have bent it into a variety of curious shapes. His hair was receding, accentuating the dome of his forehead; this and the formal clothes he wore made him seem a little older than the age of forty-six years which they had now confirmed for him.

One thing was added to the face they knew from the sketch. Although he had invited them into his own house and he sat in his favourite armchair, James Whittaker was extremely nervous. He twisted a large, clean handkerchief between his stubby fingers as he sat in the tastefully furnished modern room and saw the comfortable, ordered world in which he had lived and been successful disintegrate before his eyes.

He had got off on the wrong foot by trying to disclaim all knowledge of the dead girl. Lambert said, "Unfortunately, you are a well-known local face, Mr Whittaker. Let me explain to you why we are here this morning. We have three witnesses who saw you going in and out of the basement flat in Rosamund Street where Tamsin Rennie lived. Not on one occasion, but on several. The last one was only a few days before someone put his hands round her throat and crushed the life out of her. Do you still wish to deny that you were ever there? If so, you had better get yourself a lawyer and we'll continue this interview at the station."

The colour had drained from Whittaker's rather florid face with every phrase from Lambert. He must have suspected this when Hook arranged the meeting and refused to enlarge upon the reasons for it. But like most weak men, he had hoped until the last minute that things would not be as bad as they were. Now he found that they were worse: he was staggered by the extent of the knowledge the police had acquired. He had told himself that whatever happened he must be cautious. Now the only words that would come through his dry lips were a ridiculous, "I didn't kill her!"

Lambert was not disposed to let a floundering fish off the hook. "I'm glad to hear it. Why, then, have you not come forward and offered us your help in finding out who did? Miss Rennie died a week ago tonight. We put out a request for anyone who had seen her in the days before her death to come forward. Yet if we hadn't unearthed your name from other sources, I don't believe you would ever have spoken to us."

Whittaker had twisted the handkerchief into a dry rope between his anxious fingers.

"I wanted to come and speak to you. I felt I should do. I knew it was my public duty. But I have more to lose than anyone else."

Lambert noted that mention of others, wondered how much Whittaker knew about the other men who had visited Tamsin Rennie. He would come back to that, eventually. Unless, of course, this pitiable man offered them enough for an arrest in this very room. "When did you first meet Tamsin Rennie, Mr Whittaker?"

"A long time ago now." He spoke like a bomb-blast victim, as though he could scarcely believe it was his own voice that was giving this information, "A year ago. Just a week over the year." He sounded as if the time belonged to another, half-forgotten world, much further away than the time implied.

"Where was this?"

"I saw her for the first time in Brown's Bookshop. I was buying a book about local history. It's an interest of mine. I wanted a detailed account of what happened to Hereford during the Civil War. Tamsin was very helpful to me, and surprisingly knowledgeable about other books which were out of print but perhaps available second-hand."

It was a touching glimpse of the dead girl in the world of her lost innocence, the kind a parent might have seized on and treasured. But not the mother or the stepfather of this girl, who were both at present suspected of her murder. Lambert said, "And you arranged to see her again?"

"Not on that occasion. But I ordered a book, and it was Tamsin who rang me to say that it had come in and to suggest a couple of other volumes she thought might be useful. When I went to collect the book, I asked her if she'd let me buy her lunch because she'd been so helpful. It was this time last year, a blazing hot day. We ate outside, in the garden behind the White Hart." He delivered the details with an air of wonder, clinging to the picture his words evoked.

Lambert could not stay in that time of lost innocence. He prompted, "And things moved on from there."

"Yes. We had a drink one night in a pub, just after she'd finished at the bookshop. She caught me looking round, trying to see if anyone was noticing us. I had to explain to her that I was well known, had been a local councillor for seven years. Although I was a widower, people would still gossip, if they saw me with a young girl. She was quite shy about it, but she said that if I liked we could meet in her flat – she'd only just moved in then, and she seemed rather proud of the place."

"And so you started an affair."

James Whittaker looked resentful at this brutal interruption of his wistful idyll. "Yes. I suppose we did. She used to call me Milburn, because she knew I had to keep things secret. Eric Milburn, I think. It was a bit of a joke between us, the secrecy."

Lambert smiled sourly. It was the name Tom Clarke had given them for the dead girl's older lover, the one she had obviously used to him to keep Whittaker's name a secret. The team had spent a lot of fruitless hours in following up the Milburns on the electoral register. He said abruptly, "When did you first sleep with Miss Rennie?"

The rope of handkerchief had become static as Whittaker recalled the exciting days when a young girl had declared she was attracted to him, when each step into her world had seemed like a dream. Now it began to twist again as he was recalled to his nightmare. "Tamsin took me to bed two months after we had first met."

Spare me the account of how wonderful it seemed, thought Lambert, I've heard it all before. As if he read his questioner's thoughts and sought to surprise him, the man twisting the handkerchief said suddenly, "I wasn't the only one, you know. Well, I assume you do, by now, but I want you to know that Tamsin didn't deceive me. I owe her that."

He was a strange mixture of idealism and world-weary honesty, this man. Or seeming honesty, Lambert reminded himself. Unless he was going to confess to the crime, every one of his statements would need to be weighed for their truthfulness, in due course. He said, "Tamsin took money from you for sex, didn't she?"

He saw Whittaker's face wrestling with the idea of his special girl as a prostitute, thought of the lurid headlines the popular press would build from the brutal facts of his situation, and shuddered inwardly for him. Eventually Councillor James Whittaker said, "No. Not for sex. Not just like that. I gave her money, willingly. Not always at the time when we had been in bed together."

"You're saying she didn't charge you a set price for each session in bed?"

The broad face with its pliant features winced at this. "No, nothing like that. We didn't count the number of times we went to bed. I gave her a little money, to help her out with the rent. She she said I was the father that she'd never had, but a lover too, so that she had the best of both worlds."

With a father she had never known and a stepfather who had assaulted her, that might even be true, thought Lambert. He

213

could see Tamsin Rennie, who was descending into such a turbulent life, drawing a little comfort from this gentle older man. "How much did you give her altogether?"

He shrugged hopelessly. "I don't know. About a thousand pounds, I suppose, over the months."

And the rest, thought Lambert. Well, it's going to cost you a lot more than money, now. He said gently, "You say you knew even at the time that you weren't the only one. Didn't it concern you that you were becoming more involved with a girl who was in effect a prostitute?"

Unexpectedly, Whittaker responded to the harsh word only with a bitter smile. "I threw that word at her myself, Superintendent, and worse, so don't expect to shock me with it. I don't think either she or I thought of it like that, not at first. I knew her stepfather had been to see her, more than once. I was quite glad, thinking he was just trying to repair the family rift which had led to her leaving home in the first place. Then I found that not only had he seduced her at home but that he was now coming to Rosamund Street and paying her for sex. When she confessed that to me, she told me that there were others as well. It had all happened over two or three months, when she'd lost her job at the bookshop and needed money for her rent. Some of them were random pick-ups, paying her for what they got on a one-off basis."

The handkerchief slipped through his fingers and fell to the floor; his hands went on twisting against each other with a rhythm which seemed quite divorced from his otherwise static body. Lambert pressed him relentlessly. "But you didn't finish with her when you found out about this."

"No. When she poured it all out, she seemed to be as upset and shaken as I was about what she had drifted into. I said I would help her to put things right. And I think she gave up most of the men after that."

"But there was young Tom Clarke. You knew about him?"

"Yes, I knew about Tom. A pleasant young lad, Tom."

"You didn't resent Tom Clarke?"

Whittaker didn't hurry his response. He allowed himself again that caustic, rueful smile. "On the contrary, Superintendent, I resented him bitterly. He had youth and looks on his side against — well, against what you see before you. I was insanely jealous of that young man. Whenever I saw his battered old car outside the house in Rosamund Street, I wanted to know what they had done together, how many times, how he proposed that their relationship should develop. Oh, I resented him all right!"

"But you didn't give up your affair with Tamsin? Didn't even offer her an ultimatum?"

"Oh, but I did! I told her she'd have to choose between him and me, and then never forced her to do so, because I was afraid of what she'd say. I made a fair old fool of myself, didn't I? But I was in love, you see."

That old plaintive cry which both CID men had heard so often. That old plea that the heart must rule the head, however extreme the consequences. The determination that it should be so was always more disastrous when a middle-aged man or woman held it for a younger partner. Jane King's contemptuous generalisation came back to Lambert as he looked at this shattered, well-meaning innocent: "Men always think they can reform fallen girls".

Just as two days earlier Lambert had found himself feeling that he'd like his murderer to be Arthur Rennie, now he hoped fervently that it wouldn't be James Whittaker. It was unusual for him to allow such thoughts to intrude upon his objectivity, and he brushed this one away like an irritating wasp. He said harshly, "If you talked to Tamsin about Tom Clarke, you knew he was serious about her. That he wanted to marry her and take her away from here."

Again that dismissive smile at his own credulity. Like many another man, Whittaker was wise enough to see the way the world worked for most of the time, foolish only when infatuation took over. Forced now to articulate the way he had behaved, he found his folly resounding in his own ears. "I was aware that Clarke said he was serious, but I knew he had no money, that he wouldn't be able to carry it through. I couldn't leave Tamsin to flounder with him, especially when I knew she was getting deeper into the drugs. I could have paid for treatment, could have protected her, could have nursed her back to the girl she had been when I first knew her." He was almost in tears, pleading for them to take seriously the possibility that he could have achieved this, confronting again the awful ending of this girl he had loved.

Lambert, determinedly detached, said, "You had a serious argument with Tamsin Rennie, not long before she died."

"On the Monday before she was killed, yes. It was the last time I saw her, and we had a blazing row." He stated the facts with

217

a bleak objectivity. He seemed to have recovered himself a little, to have avoided the tears which had seemed inevitable. "I asked Tamsin to go into a clinic to be treated for her addiction and then to come and live with me. She wouldn't admit that her life was running out of control and I tried to make her confront that. I think she knew that she needed help, really. There was a kind of desperation about her denials. But she didn't want to make a fresh start with me."

That was the real tragedy as far as he was concerned. Contemplating it head-on seemed to be the final ignominy for him; he stared down mournfully at his hands as they finally ceased to twist against each other. Lambert said gently, "It might not have been as straightforward as you think for Tamsin to make a fresh start, Mr Whittaker. You know she was dependent on heroin. It's an expensive habit, and there is at least a possibility that she was helping to support it by dealing in drugs herself. Did you see any evidence of that in her conduct?"

It was another painful turn of the knife in his wound. "No. She never said anything about supplying drugs to others. Not to me. She despised herself for her weakness with the heroin, hated the habit. I can't see her introducing others to the same hell."

"It may not have been a willing move on her part. It's a common way of recruitment, for those who run the drugs trade. A youngster becomes dependent, cannot do without a twice-daily fix. He or she is desperate to raise the money to buy. At that stage, someone comes along with a proposition. If they will take a little risk – supply drugs to other users and collect the payments – then they'll get their own supplies free. If you are an addict by the time the offer comes, you're in no position to refuse, because if you try to do so, the threat is that your own supply will be withdrawn."

Whittaker followed the argument with his large brown eyes wide and unblinking, as if it held a hideous fascination for him. Perhaps even now he was anxious to explore a hitherto hidden area of this girl he had found so enthralling in life. He said unwillingly, "It makes sense, I suppose. She told me she'd never be able to live round here."

"But she didn't say anything to suggest who might have been supplying her?"

"No. And she never admitted she was dealing, though I thought we'd shared everything."

"We're not even certain that she was. It's an explanation that would fit the facts, that's all." Their Drugs Squad infiltrator had thought the girl was dealing, and something in Keith Sugden's reactions had confirmed it for Lambert. He was pretty sure that suave criminal performer would have dismissed them even more summarily if Tamsin Rennie had not been on the fringe of his empire.

He leaned forward, staring Whittaker straight in his distressed, rather blubbery face. "You had a serious quarrel with Tamsin Rennie on that last Monday. Did you threaten her?"

From looking grief-stricken, James Whittaker suddenly took on a hunted look, as the implications of the question struck home. "Yes. She wouldn't listen to sense. Or to what I thought at the time was sense. I suppose I did threaten her — well, I know I did. She said there was no way out, that I should leave her to rot. When I told her that there was always a way, she laughed and said I didn't know what I was talking about. She said there was danger. That might have been the drugs business, I suppose. At the time, I just thought she was being hysterical."

"Was that what made you threaten her?"

"No. It was when she said that if she was going to make a fresh start with anyone, it would be with Tom Clarke. I lost my rag

220

completely, said the young fool couldn't possibly save her, that he didn't know what life was all about." He stopped suddenly. "Who told you about all this? Was it him?"

"No. You were heard quarrelling with Tamsin, that's all. By other people in the house."

"Yes. Well, we were certainly shouting at each other. And I threatened her."

"Exactly what did you say to her, Mr Whittaker?"

He saw Hook making notes, but went on, as if anxious to have the full record of his shame recorded before he could have second thoughts. "I said I couldn't just leave her to kill herself with drugs. I said Tom Clarke would never be able to save her, that he hadn't the will or the money to do it. When she refused to listen to me, I shouted that I would kill her rather than give her up."

He breathed heavily as he watched Hook writing. He seemed not appalled at his confession, but merely relieved that the full statement of his obsession was now complete. Lambert let a long moment elapse before he spoke again, in case there was further confession or explanation to come. Then he said quietly, formally, "Did you kill Tamsin Rennie, Mr Whittaker?"

With the confession of his infatuation

complete, James Whittaker had no resistance left. He said in a flat, dejected voice, "No. And I don't know who did. Not for certain."

The last phrase aroused their interest, as he must have known it would. But he did not look into their faces as he said it. He sat, seemingly exhausted, gazing down at his twisted handkerchief on the light green carpet, as if he saw it for the first time and wondered how it could have come there. It was Hook who said, "Where were you last Wednesday evening, Mr Whittaker?"

The corners of his lips twitched a little into what was almost a smile. Here at least he thought he had an adequate answer for them. "I was at a meeting of one of the council working parties. It was a candid exchange of views, really, to get things moving, rather than a formal meeting. It was in one of the members' houses and there were six of us there. I can give you names if you want them."

"What time did your meeting begin?"

"Half-past eight."

Too late to eliminate him from the murder. The kind of alibi, indeed, which a killer might think put him in the clear for the evening, when he was planning a death. Hook merely made an impassive note. It was Lambert who said, "Did you walk to this informal meeting?"

"I did, yes. It was no more than three-quarters of a mile from here, and it was a pleasant evening."

"I see. Did your route take you anywhere near the Cathedral?"

They could see him getting excited, though he did not seem to feel threatened by this train of the questioning. "Yes. Right past it, as a matter of fact. I cut through the Cathedral Close, walked past the Old Deanery and down St John Street."

Whittaker's excitement was palpable now. Lambert said calmly, "You must be aware that puts you very near the time and the place of Tamsin's murder. Did you see anything which might now appear significant?"

"Yes. I saw Tom Clarke's old red Ford Fiesta. Parked in one of the spaces behind the Lady Chapel."

Fifteen

Detective Inspector Christopher Rushton was uneasy. "You'll have to go, because the pair of them have seen Bert and me," Lambert had said. When Chris had looked suspiciously at Hook, the Sergeant had maintained that inscrutable face, blank but serious, which he seemed to summon up specially for occasions like this. He couldn't handle the two of them together when they were in playful mood, so without further argument he agreed to go.

The building had once proudly billed itself as the Temperance Billiard Hall, and the fading letters of the title were still faintly visible over the entrance. The venture had failed in the dark days of snooker before the television boom, unable to support itself by the profits from a bar. The hall had lain empty for a year before being taken over by the council, who were now happy to rent it at a very reasonable rate to local organisations.

"Reawaken to the Lord" was the slogan on the banner which now covered the fading red letters of the old sign. The message had sounded harmless, even worthy, to the girl who handled the bookings in the council offices, and Sarah Rennie had secured the place for the evening for a mere £5. The hall had a dusty air, but it was spacious, and it could seat up to two hundred on the stackable steel and canvas chairs which were arranged in rows with an aisle down the middle.

Chris had expected the sparse attendance which seemed to him characteristic of most modern religious gatherings. He was mistaken: by the time the meeting began at least three-quarters of the seats were occupied. The congregation – for he was already beginning to think of the audience in these terms – consisted of both the converted and those who had come to listen and digest. From the muted conversations and the greetings exchanged, it seemed to Rushton that perhaps two-thirds of those in attendance were already followers of the sect established by Arthur and Sarah Rennie.

The age split was interesting to him. The preponderance, as he would have expected, was of middle-aged to older people; he judged many of the elderly to be widows – certainly women outnumbered men by about four to one in this age group, though there were several married couples evident. There were also more young people than he would have expected, perhaps thirty in all, split fairly evenly between the sexes.

Christopher Rushton himself was now thirty-three, an erect, dark-haired figure, handsome in an austere way, though he would not have seen or desired that. Something more immediately attractive to women would have better pleased a man whose confidence had been severely dented by his divorce three years earlier. There were few people of his own age in the gathering. Sitting on the end of a row at the other end from the aisle, where he could most easily observe both the proceedings and the reactions of the audience, he felt conspicuous when he wanted to be anonymous within the crowd.

Arthur and Sarah Rennie came on to the platform together. Arthur glanced round the audience and nodded, as if confirming that the numbers were adequate for his performance to begin. He walked over to the single small table at the back centre of the stage, deposited his briefcase there, and extracted three sheets of paper from it. Sarah Rennie said in a strong, high voice, "Followers of Christ, our Pastor will now address us." Then she walked to the side of the stage, descended the four steps to the floor of the hall, and sat down in a reserved seat on the front row.

Arthur Rennie looked round his audience, offering them no word of greeting, studying them without a smile as the silence became absolute. He wore a loose-fitting ivory sweater and trousers of a very pale grey; his clothes looked almost white beneath the overhead lighting as he stood tall and erect. With his proud bearing, his dark eyes deep-set on either side of the strong Roman nose, he made an impressive figure, a religious patriarch straight from Hollywood. He walked to the front of the stage, where he stood very still for a moment, stretching the seconds of expectation.

Then, as a prelude to speech, he passed both hands backwards over his short hair, and Rushton knew with that gesture that he had been used to flowing locks, enhancing his Old Testament image. It must have been a serious decision for him to have that hair removed, in the vain attempt to avoid being recognised as a regular visitor to 17a Rosamund Street.

Rennie did not use a microphone. His fine, powerful voice did not need one, and he was well aware that the effects he made with it could only be diminished by the cheap electronics of the hall. He said in ringing tones, "Prepare ye the way of the

Lord. Make straight His paths." There followed a ringing denunciation of the modern world and the way it had obscured those paths. Then came a radical dismissal of established Churches and the way they had faltered and compromised until they had eventually become deaf to the message of the Lord. The established faiths in Britain were at best fumbling and mistaken, at worst definitely harmful in their deliberate perversion of the message which had once been clear.

It was obviously an opening he had used many times before, but it was delivered with a ringing sincerity, employing a series of cadences which emphasised to perfection the arguments of this impressive revivalist. He moved on to more personal recollections. "There is more joy in Heaven over one sinner returned to grace than over a million pious prayers. Brethren, I say unto you that I am that sinner. I stumbled in the darkness and was lost. But then the Lord heard the voice of one crying in the wilderness and spoke to me. And I heard. And now I bring the Lord's message to you. And I say to each one of you: Will you hear me? Will you heed the message of the Lord? Or will you be Judas? Heeding the word and denying it? Pretending to embrace the Lord when life is easy, then kissing him and delivering Him into the arms of his enemies when life is difficult?"

Rushton was struck anew by the contrast between this undoubtedly effective public performance and that of the man who had been broken down so comprehensively by Lambert and Hook at the station. They had confronted him with his lies, of course, and got him on the wrong foot to start with, and those two were old hands at the interview game. Nevertheless, Chris had not been prepared for the charisma this man carried with him in his public persona. He was like one of those actors who is diffident in private life but dominates a stage as soon he strides on to it.

For Rushton could now feel that stirring of approval, that noiseless, intangible excitement which runs only through a live audience and makes the mass more strong than the individual. Chris was vague about his own faith: he thought he was still a Christian, but he felt here the pull of certainty, the attraction of a man who knows, not thinks, and injects you with his own conviction. Rennie might almost have been speaking to him when he went on, "Christ instructed his apostles: 'Go ye and teach all nations, baptising them in the name of the Lord.' Brethren, most of us here tonight were baptised many years ago, but we have forgotten the message of faith. We need to be born again, to be re-converted to the ways of the Lord. To learn again his message and then go forth to implement it."

After a little more in this vein, Rennie asked his audience to pray with him, converting them in that moment into the congregation which they had always seemed to Chris Rushton. "There is no need to kneel. Bow your heads and the Lord will hear you," he said. Nevertheless, he fell dramatically to his knees, placed his clenched hands beneath his chin and looked to the roof of the battered building. He was like a figure in a pre-Raphaelite painting as he intoned, "O Lord, make us proof against the ways and the temptations of the wicked world which is everywhere around us. Give us the strength to reject the comforts of this world, the diversions of pleasure and possessions."

Rennie remained on his knees as he looked out across the rows of expectant faces. He appeared surprised to see them there, as if he had forgotten them in the raptures of prayer. Then he said, "Let us take a moment of private prayer to dedicate ourselves to the service of the Lord." He knelt very erect, with his head thrown back, his eyes closed and his hands clasped in rapt concentration.

A minute is a long time in these circumstances. When Rennie rose easily to his feet and smiled for the first time at the faces in front of him, there was an electricity of expectancy in the air. "Brethren, I feel you are with me. I feel your faith lifting me, carrying me forward. Believe me, it is the finest feeling I know in this wicked world of ours. I am receiving it, and it lifts me; but it is you who are giving it, and I say unto you that in matters of faith it is always better to give than to receive."

Chris Rushton had noticed a young man three seats away to his right getting more and more agitated through this performance from the platform. At first Chris thought he was merely affected by the message, a youngster finding faith and anxious to manifest it publicly. Now he realised that this was the only person in the hall who was displaying a resistance to this message. The man could not have been more than twenty-three or four. He now leapt to his feet as if driven beyond control by the preacher's last phrase. "You know a lot about receiving, Rennie! *And* about taking. From old ladies!"

There was a collective gasp from the audience, an outraged shushing from the sea of faces which turned to see whence this sacrilegious outburst had come. From the

231

eminence of his platform above them, Rennie held up his arms. "Brethren, let him speak. It is not his own wickedness that we hear but the wickedness which an evil world has bred into him!"

Rennie was immeasurably more controlled and articulate than his challenger, who struggled to speak in the glare of collective hostility turned suddenly upon him. The young man shouted, "You had my grandmother's savings! She signed away her savings to you, you cheat! Then you made her make a will to give you her house."

Rennie held up a single hand, palm towards the youth. "I do not know who you are, young sir, and I do not wish to know. Anything that has been done has been done willingly and in full knowledge. Those who follow the ways of the Lord often wish to divest themselves of possessions to bring themselves closer to Him. If they see ways in which his work can be helped, they devote what little they have to assist that work. My son, you should applaud them for that, not denigrate them."

The young man seemed to be disconcerted by the calm way this crime had been asserted to be a virtue, by the way he had been accused of denigrating the grandmother he had sought to protect. He had a shopping bag on the seat beside him, from which he dragged some sort of document that he now waved vaguely at the platform. "She didn't know what she was doing! She was an old lady, whose mind was going a little. An old lady who you took advantage of, who would never—"

"You are interrupting our worship, young man. If a relation of yours has chosen to devote her resources to furthering the work of Christ, I applaud her!" He looked round the audience that he had turned into a congregation. "I don't think anyone here would accept that I had gained anything personally from any diversion of wealth from Mammon to the work of the Lord. Those who know me, those whom I regard as my friends, would see any such suggestion as preposterous. But perhaps you are not suggesting any such thing. I should be loath to judge you guilty of such sin. But my son, you are interrupting our prayers. I shall be happy to discuss any misunderstanding with you in private at the end of the evening, when I hope we shall be able to kneel together and pray as one to the Lord."

Rushton, who had sensed that the questioner was not going to survive this confrontation, had scribbled on a page torn from his diary, "Contact DI Rushton, Oldford CID". As the young man now pushed past him and made his exit, he pushed the scrap of paper swiftly into his shopping bag. Full of incoherent fury, the youth shouted from the back of the hall. "You're a cheat and a villain, Rennie, and the world is going to hear about it!" Then he fled from the hall and the scene of his failure.

All eyes turned back to Arthur Rennie. He had moved to the side of the stage to address his critic, and now he stood there immobile for a moment, still as a statue, with a face full of sorrow. Then he shook his head unhappily from side to side, moved back to the centre of the stage, and stood like a Messiah in his ivory clothes beneath the central light. He intoned, "O Lord, we pray that Thou wilt forgive Thy errant servant, who has seen fit to insult Thy name and Thy works here tonight. Forgive him, Lord, for he knows not what he does."

There was a ragged chorus of Amens from the crowded seats in front of Chris Rushton. The DI was astounded how small had been the impact made by the single dissenting voice in this gathering. The skill with which it had been handled seemed to have increased rather than diminished the stature of the central figure in the scene. Rennie now succeeded in identifying himself even more closely with the God they wanted to worship, through a series of prayers which followed. Rushton recognised scraps of the Book of Common Prayer, fragments of the Roman Catholic Mass, even at one stage a couplet that he was sure originated in Shakespeare rather than the Bible. But the dominating source was the Old Testament, and the dominating figure in this mish-mash was the Old Testament prophet who bestrode it and drove it, as Moses had bestridden and driven an earlier charismatic movement.

It was by any standards a skilful performance. Rushton had in his time arrested successful con men, had testified against them in court, and had always found them seedy individuals, who deceived vulnerable and pathetic, usually elderly, people and milked them of their savings. This man handled a mass audience with the skill of a stand-up comic, though his intentions were deadly serious. And like a comedian, he came alive with an audience, fed off it, became something larger and more dangerous in tandem with it than he was in a one-to-one situation. The seducer and hypocrite, whom Lambert and Hook had exposed so quickly when he was alone, was a different proposition here, in what Chris was forced to admit was his natural element.

By the time he came to what was clearly,

to a cynical policeman, the real business of the evening, he had his audience eating out of his hand. In the first few minutes of his address, Sarah Rennie and a woman at the other end of the front row had instigated the audience participation by their own enthusiastic responses to the Pastor's rhetorical questions from the platform. But the rest of the rows did not need much prompting. They had moved from a gathering chorus of alleluias to repeating the prayers after their leader, until in the end they sought to out do each other in their demonstrations of fervour.

Chris had been waiting to hear the request for money he knew must surely come. But it struck no jarring note with this audience when it did. Looking along the rows of rapt faces, Rushton saw few that were troubled by the switch: for them, the transition from prayers to monetary demands was clearly a seamless one. Rennie moved from a denunciation of the worship of the false God of Mammon to a generalised account of the dangers of wealth and opulent living. He quoted the story of the young man whom Christ told to sell all his possessions if he wished to become a disciple.

Then he brandished a finger on an outstretched arm, Gladstone-like, at his audience and intoned the quotation Chris had been waiting for as if it came newly minted from his fertile mind: "Brethren I say unto you, It is harder for a rich man to enter the gates of heaven than it is for a camel to pass through the eye of a needle." He paused, lowering his arm in slow motion to his side. "Harder than for a camel to pass through the eye of a needle. In other words, impossible. Think on that, brethren." Some echoed the word "impossible". The hissing sibilants passed like a whispered message along the rows. Others shouted "Alleluiah!" and nodded at each other in the discovery of this sombre truth.

Rennie was suddenly quieter, intensely serious. "That is why I do not apologise as others might for divesting you of money and possessions. In the harsh and evil world in which we live, the Word of the Lord cannot be spread without resources. It is glorious work, brethren, and money cannot be better spent. But the reason I do not apologise for asking for your support is that I am offering you the chance to tread securely on the narrow path which leads to Heaven. Only those who divest themselves of the possessions of this world can hope to enter the Kingdom of Heaven. Brethren, I am offering you tonight the chance to take the first faltering steps along that road. And

I say unto you, once you have stripped away the dross of possessions, once you have divested yourself of the fool's gold that sinful men take as the trappings of success, your tread along the path of virtue will become stronger and surer, until it becomes a triumphant march. And in the end, it is we who have forsaken the trappings of this life who will march together towards Salvation!"

His wife and his other front-row acolyte now passed collection plates along the rows of the audience. Rushton saw Sarah Rennie flick a ten-pound note into the plate as she transferred it from the first row to the second, and there was a good deal of paper money amidst the pound coins by the time the platters had completed their journey.

Arthur Rennie had remained on the platform throughout these minutes, kneeling in prayer, transformed into an image of Christ in the Garden of Gethsemane. Nor was he foolish enough to finish on the note of acquisition. He rose again to his full height, congratulated his audience upon their taking this opportunity to divest themselves of what he called "the dross of Satan", and led the way in prayers which united them in an emotional commitment to "the Lord and His paths, which had seemed lost but are now revealed once again unto us". The date and place of the next meeting were announced and enthusiastically received.

Many of his followers remained to talk at the end of the formal proceedings. Covenant forms were produced for those who sought to regularise their commitment, while Sarah Rennie offered her services to two elderly enthusiasts who sought to revise their wills to aid the work of the Pastor.

It was a good half-hour after the formal ending of the meeting before Detective Inspector Chris Rushton was able to have the Rennies to himself. It was Rushton who had prepared the formal statements for them to sign as summaries of their exchanges with Superintendent Lambert, but they had seen him only very briefly. Sarah Rennie had tipped the contents of the collection plates into a copious handbag by the time Rushton emerged from the shadows of the now-darkened hall to the platform at the front which was still brightly lit. They seemed surprised to see him, but Chris was sure that Arthur Rennie at least had been aware of his patient, watchful presence in the shadows.

"I am Detective Inspector Rushton from Oldford CID. And that was an impressive performance, Mr Rennie," said Chris. "You had them eating out of your hands by the end, didn't you?"

Rennie refused to take offence. "The Lord speaks, not me, Inspector Rushton. He expresses himself through me: I am merely his channel. If you are saying that on this occasion those who were drifting along the paths of unrighteousness saw the error of their ways, then I am gratified."

"Gratified to the tune of several hundred pounds, from what I saw. With the prospect of more to come, from covenants and legacies. Quite a profitable business, evangelism. For some."

"Whatever we collect will be diverted swiftly to the work of the Lord," said Sarah Rennie stiffly.

"I wonder whether the people of East Sussex would agree with that," said Rushton.

The reaction was disappointing. He had expected bluster, denials, indignation. Instead, Arthur Rennie said quickly and calmly, "We have nothing to answer for to you about East Sussex, Inspector. If you have anything more to say on the subject, then charge us. Otherwise, the subject is closed."

" 'Put up or shut up', as they say. Well, you know that the police there haven't a case to take to court."

"Then I suggest you leave the matter, Inspector Rushton, before you get yourself into trouble with the laws of slander," said Rennie.

Arthur Rennie had collected considerable sums of money in the area around Chichester by mounting a revivalist campaign on the lines of his present "Mission to Herefordshire". There had been copious gifts from ageing widows, deeds of covenant a-plenty, and two useful legacies. The police had prepared a case and been ready to move. Then one of their key witnesses, a ninety-one-year-old man who had been tricked into making a gift much larger than he intended, had died suddenly and inopportunely of natural causes, and two others had been bought off by having most of their money returned. No one enjoys going into court and saying under oath that he has been a gullible fool, and that makes it difficult to mount a case against people like the Rennies. The case had collapsed like a house of cards, and now Arthur Rennie was bold enough to taunt Rushton with that knowledge.

The DI said hastily, "I wanted to talk to you about a much more serious crime. The murder of your daughter, Tamsin Rennie."

Sarah Rennie bristled with anger. "We have said all we have to say about Tamsin. She was a child of Satan, and it is with Satan that she will now spend eternity."

"She was your child, Mrs Rennie. And it was not Satan but some human being who is still walking about the streets of our city who killed her and has to be apprehended for that crime."

"And what is that to do with us?"

Rushton resisted the impulse to say that any mother must surely be concerned to locate her daughter's killer. They had been down that road before; it led nowhere that was profitable. "I wish to check out some of the details of your statements." He made it plural, hoping to imply that their statements contradicted each other at some points, though there were in truth no significant differences. "We have now interviewed over fifty other people, and you may be able to illuminate some things for us."

Arthur Rennie said coolly, "Inspector, it seems to me you may be casting your net over too small an area, if you are presuming that Tamsin's murderer is walking free on the streets of Hereford. As I understand it, she was involved with drugs. Was, I believe you told us, a heroin addict. Surely that means it is possible that her killer comes from that violent world, which stretches far beyond the walls of Hereford."

It was cool and reasoned, far removed from the high-blown Messianic vein in which he had conducted the public part of the evening. A calculating, intelligent opponent, this man; Rushton was interested to note that his only comment so far on the death was to point to something which led suspicion away from him and his extraordinary wife. Chris said, "That is a fair enough point. How much do you know of Tamsin's addiction and its consequences?"

Sarah Rennie said fiercely, "Nothing! We did not want to know of it. She defied us and cut us off when she sold her soul to Satan."

Rushton said, almost as if she had not spoken, addressing his question directly to Arthur Rennie, "We now know that she was dealing in drugs. Have you any idea who her supplier might have been?"

"No." Was it someone coming to her flat in Rosamund Street?"

"That would be unusual, but not impossible. The short answer is that we do not know, as yet. Did Tamsin herself give you any indication, perhaps unwittingly, of who might have been providing her with drugs? It's likely, you see, that the same person eventually provided the supplies for her to sell on."

"No." His answer came promptly, too promptly, and Rushton realised that he was anxious to prevent any discussion of his own visits to his dead stepdaughter. "What

243

about this boyfriend she seemed to have acquired, this actor or whatever he was?"

"Tom Clarke? No. We've questioned him extensively, and are satisfied that he has no connections with the supply of heroin."

"Then I we can't help you any further. That's right, isn't it, Sarah?" He invoked his wife nervously, at odds with his previous confidence, anxious to be rid of this line of questioning, and Rushton was certain in that moment that the wife knew nothing of her husband's sexual encounters with her daughter.

Sarah Rennie said harshly, "My daughter ceased to be mine over a year ago. She had become an instrument of the devil, using her flesh to further the designs of Satan. Now we hear that she was using illegal substances to further her evil pleasures and descend deeper into the pit of hell. Do not ask me to show compassion for her. I showed her the paths of righteousness, and she rejected them."

"That does not prevent you from showing her some compassion in death. Surely you would wish whoever killed her to be brought to justice?"

There was a burning intensity about Sarah Rennie as she said, " 'If thy right hand scandalise thee, cut it off '. She scandalised me, and I cut her off."

She's driven by the same fanatical fury as those masochistic saints who enjoyed torturing their own flesh, thought Chris. She genuinely believes all this claptrap, genuinely worships the man who has brought it to her. Arthur Rennie is a charlatan through and through, but this mistaken woman is that most dangerous of creatures, a fanatic who believes she has discovered the truth.

Rushton turned to Arthur Rennie and said, "We're checking again on everyone's whereabouts at the time when Tamsin died. I believe that you claim to have been at home with your wife on the evening of Wednesday, August 17th."

"Not claim, Inspector Rennie. I was. We even watched a little television. A thing we rarely do, but it pays us to be acquainted with the ways of the world we spend so much of our time fighting. And some of the programmes are innocent enough, if trivial and demeaning to the human spirit. In fact, we watched *Coronation Street* that night, purely because it is the soap opera most popular with the people of this country. It seemed innocent enough, though much of the action is set around a back-street public house. A girl who owned a newsagent's shop married her boyfriend, much to the disgust of nearly everyone around them, so far as I could gather. Later on we watched a documentary programme about the conflict between Russia and Germany in the 1939–45 war. *The Descent into Hell*, someone called it, and it was indeed grim stuff. A warning of the evil that lurks in all human beings."

He's giving me the documentation of their evening, thought Rushton, though I haven't asked him for it. The two of them have rehearsed this. I wonder what they are trying to hide. He said, "Are you saying that you were at home from early in the evening?"

"Yes. From six o'clock onwards." This was Sarah Rennie, at her husband's side, with her hand on his forearm.

"And you didn't go out again that night?"

"No." This formidable creature was suddenly almost skittish. "If you must know, Inspector, we went to bed early that night. We enjoyed each other's bodies. Sex may be a weakness, but within the bond of marriage it is an innocent one. The Lord gave us our bodies, and the Lord is happy that we should enjoy each other. Arthur and I were in bed before ten that night." She entwined her arm in her husband's, looked up into his face for a moment as he smiled down at her, and then gazed steadily back at Rushton. Her dark eyes glittered with pleasure in the pale oval of her face at the thought of her husband's body.

DI Rushton found her smile the most disturbing of all the strange things he had seen that evening.

Sixteen

The Sacristan had been caught. The man who had committed the serial murders of four women around Shrewsbury was in custody.

Lambert heard the official announcement of the news on the radio on Thursday morning, but it was clear that the information had been released to the press on the previous evening. SACRISTAN IS ARRESTED was all his *Times* had to offer in its headline, but the other papers were less restrained. They recalled the sexual assaults and the bizarre arranging of the bodies in country churchyards, then went on to remind the world that "the whole of the West Country, which has suffered under the Sacristan's reign of terror, will sleep more easily tonight".

They were driven to recall the retrospective horrors, for they had no details yet of the man arrested, though they speculated that he was a local resident. Desperate for copy, deprived now of the suspense and fear they had built for weeks around the hunt for the Sacristan, the fourth estate turned to another dramatic mystery, which had the advantage from their point of view of being still unsolved.

"Attention is now turning to the Copycat Killer, the man who aped the methods of the Sacristan and deposited his victim so daringly on the altar of the Lady Chapel in Hereford Cathedral last week. Police were last night still baffled about the identity of the man who chose to tease them by imitating the macabre methods of the Sacristan. Top Cop Superintendent John Lambert and his extensive team remain tight-lipped and uncommunicative about his investigation, which we understand has so far come up against a wall as stout and unyielding as that of the Cathedral itself."

There was more in the same vein, and some of the tabloids repeated their dramatic pictures of the scene of the discovery of Tamsin Rennie's body to accompany their theme of police bafflement. All good knock-about stuff, but it would no doubt turn nastier if there was no arrest in the next few days, thought Lambert, as he drove to work.

He looked at his watch as he went into the Murder Room at Oldford CID on the morning of Thursday, August 25th. It was exactly a week to the minute since the body had been discovered on the altar of the Lady Chapel.

Lambert decided it was time to put a little pressure on Thomas Clarke, apprentice actor and murder suspect. He called him into the Oldford CID headquarters, had him ushered into an interview room, and left him to kick his heels there for twenty minutes.

Tom had been directed into a spot in the walled car park of the police station when he arrived. Whilst he waited in the window-less room to find out why he had been summoned, a sergeant and two constables examined the seats and the boot of his car for any sign that the body of Tamsin Rennie had rested there. By the standards of the forensic experts, it was a cursory search. But the two men and the woman knew what they were looking for: principally, fibres from the clothing the dead girl had worn when discovered in the Lady Chapel, and secondly, any other chance evidence that had fallen from the dead girl and gone unnoticed. Serendipity can help detection as it aids other facets of life, but you have to help it along by diligent searching.

If anything to suggest a connection with the body was found in this unofficial search of the vehicle, the car would be passed on to the forensic crime laboratory staff for a more detailed and systematic searching. The sergeant and the constables found nothing significant. The car was splashed with the mud of the country lanes of Herefordshire on the outside. Its interior had been thoroughly cleaned at some time in the last few days.

Tom Clarke sat in the ten foot square airless room with the single bulb set behind a wire cage in the low ceiling and became more nervous. On the watch he consulted too frequently, the minutes ticked blank and busy. That was a quotation from somewhere, he thought, probably some poem from the First World War. He cudgelled his brains to try to pinpoint the source, but the answer would not come, and the attempt to divert his mind from his present predicament failed.

They knew the big thing he had concealed. He felt certain of that. But how much more did they know, or fancy they knew, about him and Tamsin and what had happened last week? His palms were sweating. He found that however much he rubbed them on his handkerchief or the sleeves of his jacket, they were moist again within seconds.

Beyond the walls of this room, which seemed at every moment more like a prison cell, he could hear muffled sounds. The bleeping of telephones; shouts of enquiry down an unseen corridor; the opening of drawers in metal filing cabinets; the sound of voices, calling words he could never distinguish; the sound, twice, of female laughter. He wondered how much of this activity revolved around him, how much of it was preparation for the ordeal he was now sure was in store for him.

He speculated on who would confront him across the small table which was screwed to the floor. Probably it would be different men from the grave Superintendent and the burly Sergeant who had listened to him so attentively at his first interview. He rather hoped it would be, if he was to be confronted with his lies. It would be less embarrassing if it was different people; he might even be able to make out it was some kind of misunderstanding, that the wires of exchange had been a little crossed.

It was the same men.

Tom stood up automatically when the door of the room finally opened and the two big plain-clothes officers came briskly into it. He was ready to shake hands, to smile and be smiled at, to begin the exchange in a civilised manner. They scarcely even looked at him until they were sitting opposite him on the other side of the table. Then he thought their eyes looked like those of lions surveying a tethered goat. The weather-beaten sergeant pushed a cassette into the tape recorder at the right-hand edge of the table and said, without taking his eyes off his prey, "Second interview with Thomas Clarke, Thursday, August 25th at ten eighteen. Present: Superintendent Lambert and Detective Sergeant Hook."

Lambert looked at Tom for a long ten seconds before he said, "You were less than honest with us when we talked to you last Saturday, Mr Clarke."

Tom, usually so ready with words, found now that he could not produce them. He faltered eventually into, "I don't know what you mean," and then immediately regretted it. He had put on the leather jacket his mother had bought him under careful guidance for his last birthday. His friends had joked about the macho image the jacket gave him; he felt anything but macho here, isolated under the relentless scrutiny of two men who were professionals in a world which was alien to him.

Lambert did not smile. "Help the boy, Sergeant Hook," was all he said.

Hook flicked open the pages of his loose-leaved notebook, referred to the information he knew by heart, and looked back into the pale, handsome face. "You said that you were at home on the evening of Wednesday, August 18th."

"Did I?"

Hook studied him for a moment, then dropped his eyes to his notebook. "To be precise, you said: 'I was at home. I'd spent the day decorating and I was knackered. I tried to ring Tamsin at about eight o'clock, but there was no reply.' There were no witnesses to this; your mother was at a yoga class, you said."

Hell, thought Tom. It seemed worse, with all that detail he had thrown in to make the lie convincing. He could hardly say it was a simple mistake, that he had got his nights mixed up, when he had thrown in that bit about ringing the flat at eight o'clock and getting no reply from Tamsin. He said, "I'd like to change my statement. I -- I was mistaken."

Lambert said, "We don't believe that, Mr Clarke. You must take us for fools if you think we might."

"Yes. Well, I'd better tell you where I really was on that night, then, hadn't I?" Tom attempted a dismissive laugh, but none came. "May I ask who informed you that I was not at home that night?"

"No, Mr Clarke, you may not. And I should remind you that you are now in the position of having told us a deliberate lie in a serious crime inquiry. A crucial lie, because it was an attempt to establish an alibi for the time of a murder. You have wasted quite enough of our time. You had better tell us immediately where you were and what you were doing on that Wednesday evening."

"I was in the Cathedral. In the nave of the Cathedral, to be exact. With two hundred other people. Rehearsing for the Three Choirs Festival. We sang for over two hours There was one chorus we couldn't get right. We tenors were too strident, the conductor told us." He wanted to go on and on, with fact after innocent fact. While he was talking they could not press him. And they did not interrupt, but merely studied him, as if his behaviour under stress was a matter of captivating interest to them. But eventually he had to come to a stop.

Lambert said, "You will understand that once you have lied to us, we shall treat each one of your subsequent statements with caution. How did you get to this rehearsal?"

"I came by car. In my little old Fiesta. Well, it's my mother's actually, but she lets me use it almost whenever I need it. She's very—"

"Where did you park this vehicle?"

"In the car park at the rear of the Cathedral. It's private really, for Cathedral employees, but they don't mind members of the choir using it in the evenings."

"Behind the Lady Chapel, in fact."

Tom felt the colour draining from his face. "Yes. Yes, I suppose it is, right behind the Lady Chapel."

"Within a few yards of the spot where Tamsin Rennie's body was discovered the next morning. We've inspected the spot where your Fiesta was parked, Mr Clarke. It is thirty yards from the St John's door entrance to the Cathedral at the rear. The nearest access to the Lady Chapel. We've measured the distance exactly: it might prove to be important, to someone carrying a body."

"Yes. Yes, I suppose so, but but that is the entrance that all the choir members use for evening rehearsals. It's left open when the main door and all the other entrances to the Cathedral are locked at the normal time, you see."

"You were parked in the spot nearest to the St John's door. You must have been there early to get that."

"Yes. I was there thirty-five minutes before the rehearsal was scheduled to begin."

"Because you had a body to dispose of ?"

256

"No! That's ridiculous. I wanted to marry Tamsin. To take her away from all her troubles and—"

"And she was resisting that idea, Mr Clarke. Becoming more and more a slave to heroin. Supplying heroin to others, becoming a dealer, with all that that implies. Perhaps choosing to make her future with another man rather than with you. And so you killed her, in your frustration that she would not do what you wanted."

"No! No, I didn't! You must see that I would never have killed my Tamsin." Tom found himself almost weeping in his need to convince them.

Lambert's voice went on steadily, inexorably. "No. I don't see that. I see certain facts, Mr Clarke. I see that you secured for yourself the parking spot from which you could most easily transfer a body weighing one hundred and ten pounds to the Lady Chapel. And with the least danger of being detected in doing so. I see that you lied about all this when we spoke to you five days ago; that you directly misled us; that you fed us information which has delayed the progress of a murder inquiry."

"I know. That's all true. But I didn't kill Tamsin."

"Then you had better set about convincing us of that. Why did you tell us you were at home on that Wednesday evening, when you were in fact in the very place where the body had been found?"

"I was stupid. I knew when I saw you that the body had been found in the Lady Chapel. And I knew that the boyfriend is always a suspect. I thought if I told you that I'd been around at both the time and the place of the killing, you'd not look any further for a murderer."

"You underestimate us, Mr Clarke. In more ways than one. You don't know much about the thoroughness of a murder hunt if you thought you were going to get away with that." He spoke witheringly, but he was uncomfortably conscious that they had been made aware of Clarke's presence in the Cathedral on that fatal evening not by diligent police work but through the chance observation of his car by another suspect in the case. A police officer had been pursuing the tedious task of checking out the hundreds of choristers involved in the rehearsal for the Three Choirs Festival, just in case any of them had connections with the dead girl, but no one so far had come to him with Clarke's name. Lambert said, "Have you always sung in the Cathedral choir?"

"No. I sang as a youngster, then went off to RADA. I can't be a regular member because well, because when I'm working,

I'm obviously not available for rehearsals in the evenings. But six weeks ago someone said if I was 'resting', they were short of tenors for the Three Choirs Festival. I jumped at the chance. I was lucky to get in like that, and I've thoroughly enjoyed it." Just for an instant, he had forgotten his perilous situation in the joy of making music.

Possibly he isn't on the official lists, thought Lambert. Amateur organisations are notoriously tardy with the paperwork. Cancel the rocket to the DC combing through that list. He said heavily, "You had better tell us exactly what you did that evening; accurately this time, please, and with nothing conveniently omitted. Begin with why you were parked in such an advantageous position behind the Cathedral, thirty-five minutes before the rehearsal began."

"I went early because I hoped to have a few words with Tamsin. I parked there because I thought I'd secure my parking spot at the Cathedral before the others turned up. It can be chaos just before the time we begin the rehearsal, as you can imagine. And it's only five minutes down St Ethelbert Street to Tamsin's flat in Rosamund Street, as you know."

"And did you see Tamsin?"

"No. The last time I saw her was on

259

Tuesday morning after I'd stayed the night, as I told you on Saturday. I didn't lie about that. But what I didn't tell you properly was that we'd had a row. She was saying that she wouldn't come away with me, that it was all hopeless, that she'd need to finish with me. I couldn't leave it like that. I wanted to have another go at her, make her see reason."

"And so you went to her flat on that Wednesday night?"

"Yes. But she wasn't there. There was no light on when I got there."

Hook, trying not to sound too excited over his notebook, asked, "What time was this?"

"Seven o'clock. Perhaps a little after that."

"Did you go into the place? We know you have a key."

"Yes. Just to make sure she wasn't there. She sometimes — you know, with the heroin, she sometimes "

"Passed out, I know. Or lost all sense of time."

"Yes. But she wasn't there when I looked in. I just looked round briefly and went back to the Cathedral. I must have left the flat by seven fifteen."

Lambert studied the revealing face of the young man on the other side of the table. It was a strange combination of distress and a desperate anxiety to convince them that what he said was true. He said, "You say you looked round quickly and then went away. What was the state of the flat?"

"The state of the flat? It was well, just as it usually was."

"Tidy?"

Puzzlement was added to the other emotions which flitted across the unlined young face. "Well, no. I wouldn't say tidiness was one of Tamsin's virtues. Not, well, not since the drugs got a hold on her."

"We discussed this with you when we saw you on Saturday. So what you're now saying is that the flat was in some disorder when you looked in before you went to your choir rehearsal?"

"Yes. I'm not saying it was like a tip, mind. But there were clothes on the floor. An unwashed beaker and plate in the sink, I think. That kind of thing." He shrugged helplessly, trying to remember what he had said at their first meeting, wondering if they were trying to trap him, still not sure where this line of questioning was leading him.

Lambert told him. "I'm taking this up with you again because you admit you have lied to us about your whereabouts on the evening when Tamsin died. If what you're now telling us is true, it is significant. Tamsin was almost certainly killed in the

261

early evening of that Wednesday. It is probable that she never re-entered the flat in Rosamund Street after the time of seven fifteen which you are giving us for your visit. But the Scene of Crime team didn't find the flat in the condition you describe."

"You said that on Saturday. Do you mean that someone went in there and tidied the place at some time after her death? But why would they do that?"

Lambert found himself wishing he could see Tom Clarke in one of his stage performances. He would like to have known how convincing he could be as an actor. At the moment, he was doing a good line in wide-eyed surprise; but he was a naive young man, so it might just be innocence. He said impatiently, "We discussed this with you on Saturday. There might be a perfectly innocent reason why the flat was tidied. But being suspicious policemen looking for a murderer, we are inclined to the view that someone was trying to remove evidence which might have implicated him, or someone close to him."

"Yes, I see. You mean someone went through the place carefully to make sure there wasn't anything there which would suggest him as a killer?"

Lambert wondered how genuine this question was. They had discussed the state of the flat with him five days earlier, but it was possible he hadn't realised the full import of the questioning until now. "Indeed. The Scene of Crime team found no crockery in the sink, the carpets clean, and Tamsin's clothes neatly folded or hung. We don't know what, if anything, was removed from the place."

"No. I can see now why you think the tidiness was significant."

"You are one of several people who had keys to that flat, Mr Clarke. Did you go back there, later on that Wednesday night, or at any time on Thursday? We didn't know where Tamsin Rennie had lived until over a day after her body was discovered. I should remind you that one of the reasons for that was that you didn't come forward to tell us of your association with her until three days after her death."

"No. I didn't go back there. The last time I was in the flat was the time I've just told you about." His face had the blankness of a stubborn child's, desperately wanting to be believed, repeating statements with a blind persistence.

"You had ample time to go back there in the late evening, after your choir rehearsal in the Cathedral was over. It would have been quiet then, with very little chance of anyone seeing you enter or leave. And a light in the place would have excited no suspicion at ten o'clock in the evening."

"No. I went straight home after we'd finished."

"Without any further attempt to contact the girl you'd so wanted to see earlier in the evening? Without any further attempt to resolve the dispute you admitted having with her on your last meeting?"

"No. No, I didn't go back. And I'll tell you why. She'd have been high on heroin by that time of the night, particularly if she'd been out. There was no talking to her after a fix." He was trying desperately to convince them, and now his dejection lifted as an escape route suggested itself. "Look: you found a picture of me there, didn't you? If I'd been back and cleared away evidence of my presence, I'd have taken that away, wouldn't I?"

Lambert smiled. He had considered the matter of that highly theatrical profile picture of the man before him. "You might perhaps have removed it, yes. If you had given the matter any thought, you would have left it. We were always going to find out about a regular boyfriend, who was hoping to marry our murder victim, weren't we? To find not a single trace of you in that flat would in fact have been highly suspicious. I may say that the only one we did

264

find was that single photograph."

Tom revolved this, wanting to ridicule their thinking, finding after all that he could not refute the logic. He repeated miserably, "I didn't go back there again after seven fifteen on that Wednesday."

"Very well. Tell us what happened after the rehearsal."

His face brightened as he thought about it. There was someone who could corroborate his account of at least this part of the night. "I helped a disabled girl out to her car. We have two or three disabled people who sing in the choir. This one is a soprano. She has to sit at the front because she has a wheelchair. Her sister is a choir member too. I helped her to get Debbie out to her car. It was parked next to mine, as near to the rear entrance as they could get it. The Cathedral staff leave a ramp to get over the step at that St John's door at the rear of the Cathedral, so it's easy enough to get the chair in and out, but I was useful in helping to get Debbie into the passenger seat of her sister's car."

They sensed his relief as he piled detail upon innocent detail. Lambert said, "And after this?"

"Well, I saw Debbie and her sister out of the car park. Then I drove home myself."

"You didn't go anywhere else? See anyone

else, so that we can confirm your movements after you left the Cathedral?"

"No." His face was full of apprehension again, as he realised that what he had said about the disabled girl covered him for no more than a few minutes after the rehearsal. "What I told you on Saturday about what I'd been doing earlier in the day is true. I'd been decorating all day and I was knackered. Then we'd had a long rehearsal in the Cathedral and I was pretty well all in. In the ordinary way, I might have gone for a drink with a couple of other members of the choir, but I was exhausted. I drove straight home."

"Where you arrived about what time?"

"I couldn't be exact. I should think about ten fifteen."

"And is there anyone who can confirm this?"

"No. Again, I think I mentioned on Saturday that Wednesday is my mother's yoga class night. After I'd spoken to you on Saturday and foolishly told you that I was at home that night, I — I actually asked Mum to tell you that she phoned me at home during the evening, but she didn't do that of course, because I was at the rehearsal in the Cathedral."

"Well, your mother wasn't called upon to lie for you, because we found where you were from another source. What time did she come home on that Wednesday night?"

"She usually goes for a drink after her yoga with a couple of her friends. She wasn't in until after eleven."

"Unfortunately for you. Or fortunately, if you are still choosing to lie to us about your movements."

"I'm not. I want you to find out who killed Tamsin."

"And have you any idea who that might be?"

"No. None at all."

"Then please go away and think about it. If you remember anything you think might be significant, however tiny or peripheral you think it, get in touch with us immediately. And don't leave the area without letting us know."

Tom Clarke found his hands trembling on the steering wheel of the red Fiesta as he drove it with exaggerated care out of the police car park at Oldford. He took the quiet way back to his home, through the country lanes of Gloucester and Hereford. When he had gone no more than two miles, he pulled off the road. For a moment, he stared across the golden stubble of the cornfields to the green hills beyond them.

Then he put his face into his hands and wept uncontrollably.

Seventeen

Lambert, Rushton and Hook held a council of war late on the morning of that Thursday. It was over a week now since the body had been discovered. The press officer, under siege from hungry journalists now that the Sacristan had been arrested fifty miles to the north, was pressing them for news. They had learned much, but could not tell him that they were yet near to an arrest.

It was DI Rushton who was responsible for the correlation of information assembled from the team of thirty working on the case. "We've now got the forensic report to add to the post-mortem findings," he said. "It came in while you were talking to young Clarke, but it doesn't add a lot to what we already know. She ate fish and chips sixty to ninety minutes before death, but we're not sure of the precise time when that meal was taken: heroin addicts are notoriously random in their eating habits.

"No one saw her buying the food, nor has anyone so far admitted to seeing Tamsin

Rennie on the day of her death, but everything points to the time of death as being some time in the early evening. As the body was not found until the next morning, we have to presume that no one could have deposited it in the Lady Chapel until after the Cathedral was officially closed on that Wednesday night. It would have been too risky, with members of the public still around. That in turn means that as the rest of the doors were closed, either the living Tamsin Rennie must have been taken in by the St John's door entrance and strangled in the Chapel, or her body must have been taken through that door, perhaps whilst the rehearsal was in progress."

"Have forensic come up with anything from what the Scene of Crime team passed to them?"

"Not much that's useful. Their negative findings confirm that someone had cleaned the flat through very thoroughly in the period between the girl's death and the SOC team getting in there late on Friday afternoon. Even the chairs and upholstery had been vacuumed carefully, probably with a Dyson cleaner, they reckon."

Lambert smiled grimly. The more efficient cleaning tools became, the more was removed that might have been useful to CID. "What did Mrs King, the landlady, have to offer on that?"

Rushton shrugged. He had not met that contained and enigmatic lady, but he had heard much about her from the team. "She confirmed that neither she nor the cleaner she employs had been into the place before Jack Johnson and his team."

"And I suppose the refuse lorry had been round as usual at the wrong time for us."

It was Rushton's turn to smile. "No. They collect from Rosamund Street on Mondays. Our lads took away all the rubbish for forensic to examine. There were ten bags in all from the various residents. Must have given someone a lovely time. But they say this morning that they are satisfied that none of them contained carpet fibres or other materials matching those found in the basement flat."

So whoever had left Tamsin Rennie's rooms so clinically tidy and unrevealing had taken the detritus with them; it was no doubt hidden ever under tons of rubbish at some council tip by now. But you would have expected no less of the man who had gone to such lengths to perpetrate his elaborate imitation of the Sacristan's work. A methodical killer, this. Or killers: the unwelcome prospect of a conspiracy to defeat detection was looking a little more likely.

"Do forensic think she was killed in the Cathedral?"

"They've nothing to add to the PM report, really. No sign of murder in the flat, just as there was nothing positive in the Cathedral. But then, what would there be? No blood from a strangling, and if she was held against the floor or a chair, any fibres have been removed by our anonymous cleaner. Whoever killed her wore gloves, probably of the thick leather gardening sort, readily available from any high street store."

"So we're still not sure exactly where she died. The likeliest place would be in the Cathedral, assuming someone could get her there without her suspecting anything."

"Tom Clarke? He's the boyfriend, after all. And we now know he was in the Cathedral that night."

Lambert nodded. "And he concealed that from us. But it's not conclusive. James Whittaker was also near the Cathedral at the time of her death, and he could have suggested a perfectly plausible reason why she should meet him there."

Rushton said reluctantly, "Does that let out the Rennies? A right pair of weirdos they are. Either of them could have done it, if you ask me."

"We shall, in a minute, Chris. Let's just

spend a moment longer on the place of death. If we could put it definitely in the Cathedral, it would be a help."

Rushton shook his head. "I don't think we can, Chief. The only significant marks on the body are bruises on the back, just behind each armpit. Commensurate with the body having been lifted and moved shortly after death, the report says. It could be that someone killed her elsewhere, then put her in the boot of a car, then lugged her from there into the Cathedral via the St John's door at the rear and dumped her in the Lady Chapel."

"He'd be taking a hell of a risk of being seen, though, lugging a body about like that. Unless there was some other way of getting the body into the place, it looks much more likely that she was lured there alive and killed in an empty Lady Chapel. Don't forget she was arranged on the top step of the altar like an effigy on one of those medieval tombs, so she'd have been dragged into the right position for that little scene. The bruising behind the armpits could have been from that."

They were silent for a moment, picturing that disquieting scene in the dark and deserted Lady Chapel, each with his own figure in the role of the perpetrator of that macabre tableau. Then Lambert said,

"Right, Chris, the Rennies. You haven't reported yet on your attendance at their meeting last night."

"Right pair of weirdos, as I said! Wouldn't like either of them as a next-door neighbour. Still less as a parent."

"Crooks?"

"He is, certainly. He's taking gullible people for a ride, milking them for all they've got. My impression is that he'll move on swiftly when he's got all the major pickings from Hereford, just as he did from Sussex, and look for a new group of victims waiting to be plucked."

"Right. So we're fully convinced that he's not a genuine Christian revivalist, just working up his fervour from a real belief in a creed."

"Absolutely convinced. Oh, he's clever all right: it was an education to see him in action. I've met a few successful con men, but they've mainly been transparent liars, effective only in a one-to-one situation with people who want to believe them. Rennie was a clean-cut, impressive figure, manipulating an audience, using the euphoria of the group to carry him forward. He worked up their zeal, then rode it like a surfer on his board. And he made his pitch for their money expertly and at exactly the right moment." Rushton sounded almost enthusiastic in his recognition of skills which were so far from his own.

"Was there no one else there who saw through him?"

Rushton shrugged. "Most of them had come in search of a Christian message. They were anxious to put some kind of worship back into their lives. Arthur Rennie made it seem simple, made the issues seem clear-cut and unarguable. There may have been one or two who weren't convinced, but if there were, they went away without speaking up. Apart from one lad, who'd had some previous experience of his methods."

"He challenged him?"

"Yes. But Rennie must have met the same kind of thing before. He was ready for it, handled the lad with the same expertise he used in the rest of the meeting. Turned the feeling of his audience against his opponent, in fact."

"Did you manage to speak to this chap afterwards?"

"No. He stormed out in the middle of the meeting, when he found he was losing his battle. I couldn't speak to him without drawing attention to myself. But I managed to get a note into his bag as he left. I'm hoping he might contact me."

Lambert looked at Hook. "You see, Bert? We sent the right man. Born undercover man, Chris is. You or I would never have shown such initiative."

Rushton was never happy when these two old sweats began to have fun at his expense. He suspected that that was exactly what was going on here, but he couldn't put his finger on the right phrase to challenge. He said hurriedly, "Anyway, I didn't like Arthur Rennie at all. Be nice if we could nail him with taking money under false pretences."

"It would indeed, and hopefully we shall, especially if his victim reads his note and contacts you. However, it wouldn't make him a murderer, would it? Would you have him in the frame for his stepdaughter?"

Rushton frowned. "I'd like to. Having seen him in action, having watched the way he handled the one person who challenged him in public, I think he's pretty ruthless. If his stepdaughter was threatening to blow the gaff on him to the people whose money he'd been taking, he might just have seen her off."

Hook said, "Her challenge to him might have been even more direct. Perhaps she was just threatening to tell that strange mother of hers that her husband had been climbing into bed with her, had been visiting her in Rosamund Street for that specific purpose, in fact. Sarah Rennie's a fierce, passionate creature. I wouldn't like to be in

Arthur's shoes if she found out about that."

Lambert nodded. "She's certainly that. Do you think she's as cynical as Arthur Rennie about exploiting people's faith?"

"No." Rushton was surprised how promptly and certainly he had replied. "My impression last night was that she seems passionately in love with Arthur, and that she's a genuine zealot, carried away with the message of the Lord. A bizarre and pitiless Lord, in her case, but one she genuinely believes in. She was supporting her husband all night, doing the thankless things like starting the responses and rattling the collection plate, but I thought her loyalty came from a genuine conviction, not greed. That made her more frightening, really."

Lambert glanced at Hook, found him nodding agreement. "I think we would concur with that. The way she spoke about her daughter, her total lack of any sympathy and determination not to forgive her, were frightening, but we thought genuine. She's a fanatic, to the point of being unbalanced. I think all three of us have met fanatics who've become psychopaths. Having seen her, we're all convinced that she could have killed her own daughter, if she thought the girl was jeopardising the work of evangelism; perhaps on her own initiative, perhaps in association with her husband."

Rushton nodded slowly. "I hope it's one of the Rennies. They made my flesh creep last night. To be honest, I hope it's Arthur. If it's his wife, it will be because she's unbalanced, because she's lost all sense of reality. Then we'll have a sensational court case, the trick-cyclists will get busy, and dear Sarah will be deemed unfit to plead."

"Possibly, if she operated on her own. If Arthur Rennie's involved, we'll get him and make it stick."

Hook, despite sharing their views on the astounding Sarah Rennie, was still appalled at the thought of a mother killing a daughter, possibly because a mother had taken no part in his own upbringing. He said, "As far as we know, neither of them was near the Cathedral or Rosamund Street on the night when Tamsin was killed."

Lambert said slowly, "No, we don't. But they're each other's alibi. They say they were quietly at home that night, watching television. Arthur Rennie even volunteered details of the programmes, without being asked. Whatever we think, the husband-wife alliance is always the most difficult alibi to break. But it shouldn't prevent us from keeping them in the frame, in our own minds."

Rushton said, "What did you think of Councillor and mayor-to-be James Whittaker? He was very nervous when he signed his statement for me. But he's got every reason to be worried. The press boys are getting ready to go to town on him. His association with that girl is going to break his career in local politics, even if he didn't kill her."

Hook said, "Even with that at stake, I doubt whether he'd kill her. He seemed a fundamentally decent man, who'd got himself into a hopeless situation." Hook felt the conviction draining from his voice with the weakness of that argument.

Lambert said, "I've known more than one murderer who struck me as a decent man unable to handle desperate circumstances, Bert. People who've never been in trouble before don't know how to cope. They lose their sense of perspective and do stupid things. And even by his own account James Whittaker felt that he had more at stake than power and prestige as a local bigwig. He thought he was in love with Tamsin Rennie. He wanted to rescue her from the life she was leading. She turned him down. He had frustrated passion as well as his local standing as a motive."

Hook said, almost as though he was dragging forth the words unwillingly, "He could have got her to meet him behind the Cathedral – promised her a large sum of money, for instance. Then he could have taken her in through that door left open for the choir members and taken her into the Lady Chapel for the exchange. Killed her there, and then simply gone on his way to his meeting, which was to be his alibi for the evening."

Lambert grinned at Hook's dismay at his own suggestion. "Opportunity and motive, then. But he's not the only one. We've got a handsome young lover who lied to us about his whereabouts on the evening in question."

Bert Hook, who had decided that this handsome youth from a background so different from his own was the likeliest murderer, came in eagerly. "Tom Clarke had a better opportunity than anyone else, being in Hereford Cathedral that night for the rehearsal, and his car was parked in the slot nearest to the entrance for the Lady Chapel throughout the three most vital hours of the evening, if we accept his own revised account."

Rushton nodded. "And if we think this is a crime of passion, Tom Clarke is the strongest candidate of all. He's admitted in his revised statement that he'd had a serious row with the dead girl at their last known meeting. Not just a lovers' tiff, but a bust-up where she was threatening to end the

279

affair, whereas he still wanted to marry her and carry her off to better things." The DI spoke the last words with what was almost a sneer. Chris Rushton had become even more contemptuous of young love than most policemen since the time of his own divorce three years earlier.

Lambert looked at his taut face for a couple of seconds before he said, "You told me earlier that forensic had provided us with some news on the pregnancy."

Rushton nodded. He had wanted to save his one bit of real news for the best moment. "Two months pregnant, the PM report said, you remember. None of the people we've interviewed has declared any knowledge of her condition. We can probably presume that she hadn't told any of them about it: perhaps she hadn't been sure of it for very long herself. And perhaps it precipitated some decision that affected her situation, which in turn prompted her killer to take the action he did."

Lambert said impatiently, "Too many 'perhapses', Chris. Let's hear what forensic had to say about the pregnancy."

"The father is Tom Clarke. You can't clear everything away, even with as thorough a cleansing of that flat as was conducted after the murder. There were a couple of hairs of Tom Clarke's on one of Tamsin Rennie's sweaters which the SOC team bagged and sent to forensic: they matched them with a sample he agreed to give us when he signed his statement. Tests on the foetus have shown that the child was his."

Perhaps that had always been the likeliest answer. But CID men welcome unlikely answers: they are often significant pointers. There was a pause before Hook returned to the case against Tom Clarke. "Without forensic and the wonders of modern science, we'd probably never have known this. Probably Clarke didn't know about the pregnancy himself. But if he did and she was threatening to end the relationship, he might have lost his rag. And save for that single photograph, all the obvious traces of him had been removed from Tamsin's flat. If Clarke did kill her, he could easily have gone into the flat and cleaned it after the choir rehearsal that night; St Ethelbert Street is a quiet backwater to walk down at that time of night, and it's highly unlikely anyone, even our Nosey Parker on the other side of the street, would have seen him enter a basement flat in the darkness. We know he had a key."

Lambert said ruefully, "But then so did most of the people we regard as leading suspects. Including, probably, whoever was supplying her with drugs to sell to others.

Have we made any progress on who that might be?"

Rushton shook his head. "Not really. The team has checked out all the other residents of 17 Rosamund Street. Three of them were users of soft drugs, that's par for the course among seven mostly youngish people. But we're satisfied none of them had any connection with Tamsin Rennie. Most of them hardly knew her."

"What about the landlady, Jane King? She knows more about her residents than she admits to, I'm sure. She was much more forthcoming when we went there for a second time. She told us things about James Whittaker, for instance, that she'd withheld when we saw her soon after the murder had been discovered. Did none of the team get any more out of her?"

Rushton permitted himself a rare smile. When John Lambert had had two goes at a subject, there wasn't usually much left for anyone else to prise out. "She's a pretty tough cookie, Mrs King. But I think we've probably got as much as we're going to get, as much as she knows, perhaps. She was quite willing to talk about the Rennies and Tom Clarke and James Whittaker, whereas she hadn't been at first, as you say. But I'd be satisfied now that she's told us all she knows about them. She's even given us odd scraps that Tamsin let drop to her when she was paying her rent. But they don't add anything to what we already know."

Lambert nodded slowly. He noted Rushton's preference for the Rennies as murderers and Bert Hook's stress upon young Tom Clarke. He would have liked to make out a case for someone himself: in these informal exchanges, it helped to clarify the situation and prevent things being overlooked if people were allowed to argue for their own candidates. But he had said what he had to say about James Whittaker, reminded them that mild-mannered killers were not rare. His own fancy was for someone connected with the drugs trade; that was probably because he would be pleased if they could connect this killing with Keith Sugden and his dark empire. But the trouble was that they hadn't so far come up with any genuine contact as the person who had been providing Tamsin Rennie with her supplies of drugs to deal. It was difficult to put forward a vehement case for such a vague and faceless suspect. He said rather wearily, "Are we any nearer to establishing Tamsin Rennie's drug trade contacts?"

"Not as far as her supply goes. We've found one of the pubs where she dealt, and a kid she was supplying was brought in for possession last night. He's only eighteen.

He's been thoroughly interrogated, but we're satisfied he's no idea where Tamsin got her supplies from. He doesn't even know who's replaced her. I've been on to the Drugs Squad again this morning, but they're no nearer to giving us a supplier for Tamsin Rennie. Probably someone with a respectable front, who doesn't go anywhere near the pubs and clubs where heroin and coke get on to the streets. The secret at that level is to pass the supplies swiftly and anonymously."

"So the girl may have collected them herself rather than have them brought to her. Did she have access to a car?"

"Not as far as we know. All the suspects have transport, but they all seem genuinely innocent of any knowledge of the drugs industry. I can't see any of them lending Tamsin Rennie a car to meet her supplier. Apart from any other considerations, none of them would have wanted to get involved in the drugs trade, I'm sure. But she could have taken a taxi, if necessary. Or, more likely, collected them on foot from anywhere in Hereford."

A faceless local supplier, who might also be the person who crushed the life from Tamsin Rennie's young throat; who might have had equally anonymous assistance in depositing the body on its macabre resting place in the Cathedral. Suddenly they seemed to Lambert to have made very little progress in a week's intensive investigation.

He was left at the end of their conference with the feeling that there was something he had not exactly missed but overlooked. That somewhere, in the masses of minutiae from different areas which tumbled through his mind, there was a significant detail that he had not weighted properly.

He took Bert Hook back into his office with his notebook. In the days of old, he would have lit a cigarette. Now they had to make do with the station coffee which Bert swore had an adverse effect on his golf swing. Lambert took his first sip, grimaced, and said, "Let's just go over our exchanges earlier this morning with Tom Clarke."

Eighteen

Chris Rushton was quietly proud of his initiative in encouraging the only dissident voice at Arthur Rennie's revivalist meeting to contact him.

Rushton's strengths were organisation and thoroughness; if you needed to be sure a job would be done conscientiously and by the book, you passed it to Chris. His diligence and his computer literacy made him a valuable member of Lambert's team, filing and cross-indexing the vast amount of material which accrued from a team of thirty. This enabled Lambert to pursue his eccentric and outdated methods of leading his investigation from the front, of conducting most of the more significant interviews himself. Most modern superintendents have settled for the easy life of overview and direction from behind a desk, but as long as Lambert got results he was going to be allowed to proceed in his own archaic way.

DI Rushton had acted last night on impulse in the council hall, and apparently done the right thing when he had inserted the page torn from his diary into the young man's shopping bag as he let him past his seat. As if to emphasise that, his enterprise with that hastily scribbled message was now rewarded on the very next day. He was told that a Paul Dansen was asking for him at the front desk.

The name meant nothing to Chris, but when he went through to the reception area he recognised immediately the young man who had been so distraught on the previous evening. He had put on a suit to come to see the police; he looked uncomfortable but determined. Chris took him through to the relative quiet of his own small office beside the Murder Room.

Dansen sat on the edge of his upright chair and looked thoroughly ill at ease. It had been bad enough nerving himself to approach the front desk of a police station. Being drawn now into its mysterious inner recesses, he was already regretting his decision to follow up the note he had found that morning under the books at the bottom of his shopping bag.

Putting people at their ease was not one of Chris Rushton's strengths, but he did his best. His impulse was to talk too much himself. "Thank you for coming in so promptly, Paul. Let me start by saying that I share your view of Arthur Rennie, Born

Again Christian and self-styled Pastor of the Mission to Hereford. I believe he is deceiving people and accepting money under false pretences. I hope that you may be able to provide me with some evidence to support charges against the man. I can assure you of a more sympathetic hearing than you got from him last night at the meeting."

Paul nodded, not taking in all of this but getting the essential impression that he had done the right thing in coming here. "I want justice for my Gran, you see. Rennie makes out I'm after the money for myself, that I'm taking it away from what he calls the work of the Lord."

"You'd better begin at the beginning. Remember that all of this is new to me. Assume that I know nothing, even that I need to be convinced, if you like. Start by telling me exactly who you are. Remember, I only know Paul Dansen so far as the young man who stood up to Arthur Rennie."

Dansen hesitated, then plunged into a brief account of himself. He was a twenty-two-year-old student at the University of Gloucester. He was only in his second year of studies, because he had spent two years doing various jobs to support him on his way round the world after leaving school with his A-levels.

He was an open-faced, earnest man, who looked younger than his years, despite his experiences around five continents. He said he had met with some pretty savage treatment at the hands of the police in places as different as Africa and America, which helped to explain his diffidence in coming to Oldford in response to Rushton's scribbled invitation. The DI let him talk for a few minutes before he said, "And you say you have a complaint about the way Rennie has treated your grandmother."

Dansen nodded vigorously. "And how! I don't even know whether it's illegal or not, mind. But if it's not, it bloody well should be!"

Chris nodded encouragingly. "Quite probably it is. Let's have the details." He tapped in a heading on the new computer file he had opened. Not for him the old-fashioned notebook of Bert Hook – not when he was in his own den and could use his computer, anyway. He was only dimly aware that Hook used his notebook not just as a record but as an instrument to threaten, encourage or chasten interviewees, as the circumstances demanded. No one could produce a simple notebook with the portentous implications which Bert's timing and bearing could give to it.

Paul Dansen said, "Gran went to one of

his meetings two months ago and was duly impressed. Since then, she's given him at least three large sums of money from her building society account."

"How large?"

Paul shook his head. "I can't be sure. Hundreds, certainly. Maybe more than that. She wouldn't tell me. It's well, it's possible she doesn't know clearly herself. She used to have a mind like a razor. She taught maths at the girls' grammar school for thirty years. But she's eighty now, and this last year, she's well, her mind's gone a bit soft. She doesn't even remember what she did yesterday and who she saw "

He was almost in tears. Rushton said gruffly, "Well, it's a good thing she has someone like you to look out for her, then, Paul, isn't it?"

He nodded, fought back the tears, said, "My mum and dad live in Scotland now, so they're not around to protect her. I noticed a big difference in Gran when I came back from abroad, and since she's been ill it's accelerated rapidly."

Rushton said sharply, "Your grandmother is ill now, as well as old?"

"Yes. I'm not doing this very well, am I? Sorry, it's more upsetting than I expected it would be." He felt through the pockets of his suit, found a handkerchief, and blew his nose with vigorous relief. "She's got terminal cancer. It won't be long before it's much worse. She's going into a hospice next week. She's being very brave. When she's lucid, she says her great fear was Alzheimer's and the loss of her mind and dignity, so now she's going to avoid that."

"And you think that Arthur Rennie has been exploiting the situation?"

"I know he has. She won't show me her building society book, but I'm sure he's already been gifted most of her savings. He told her it was the Will of the Lord that the worldly dross of wealth should be used to pave the road to heaven for the righteous." Despite Dansen's distress, Rushton could hear the overblown phrases being delivered in Arthur Rennie's high rhetorical mode. "Then I found out that he'd been round there last Wednesday, exploiting her illness and her distress. I got there just after he'd gone, unfortunately. And he's refused to meet me face to face since then. That's why I was driven to interrupting his meeting and setting up last night's performance."

"He'd conned more money out of the old lady?"

"Worse than that. He's got her to sign her house away to him. He's taken away the document and I've never seen it. But I'm pretty sure it's one of those simple will forms you can buy at any stationer's, from the neighbour's description. She and her husband were called in by Gran to act as witnesses, you see."

Rushton tried to find the comfort the young man opposite him so obviously hoped for, and failed. These documents were perfectly legal, as long as the simple niceties of witnesses and signatures were observed. Rennie would surely have ensured that, for this was certainly not the first time he had pulled a trick like this. The bequest would no doubt be to some bogus religious sect with a high-sounding title, of which he and Sarah Rennie would be the officers and the only people allowed to sign cheques. It would probably even be registered as a charity, to make it more tax-efficient as a gatherer of funds like this. And this old lady might be dead within a month, by the sound of it, leaving behind only the notoriously difficult and expensive expedient of challenging a will.

Chris said, "We'll need to move pretty quickly if we're to stop him. Do you have the names of anyone else that you know is being exploited like your Gran?"

"No. I'm sure there are other people, because I gather he waved the details of other gifts and bequests before Gran's eyes when he was persuading her to sign this will. But I haven't any of the details. Gran didn't register any names, even if that bugger showed her any."

"If we can get enough from your Gran's case to have a look at the bank statements for whatever name he operates for his scams, we can probably get the names and eventually the addresses of more people, to build up the case." There might be enough from the police investigation of Arthur Rennie's activities in Sussex to persuade a building society manager to cooperate, thought Chris. The executives making financial decisions were always nervous when old people's savings were in jeopardy: no one liked the kind of publicity that could come with the exposure of a charlatan like Rennie. But Chris played it by the book, as was his wont, and didn't reveal these thoughts to the man on the other side of his desk.

Paul Dansen seemed cheered that this earnest inspector was taking his problem seriously. He said, "I could go round and try to confront him again. I've found out where the Rennies live now, by following them home after a meeting. But so far I haven't managed to see him. Usually that harridan of a wife comes out and shouts at me on the doorstep. She calls me the

Antichrist, and says I am trying to frustrate the will of the Lord. I think she actually believes it – she seems mad as a hatter to me."

Yes, thought Chris. Mad enough to kill her daughter, perhaps, if the girl got in the way of whatever strange things Sarah Rennie saw as the work of the Lord. But this distraught young man knew nothing about the involvement of the Rennies in a murder case, and it had better be kept that way. He said, "Don't go and tackle him face to face. It probably won't work and it might well make matters worse if he's put more on his guard. I can assure you that we have Arthur Rennie in our sights and that we shall be following up the case of your grandmother. Thank you for coming in to see me so promptly. I'll be in contact as soon as I have anything to report, probably within the next few days."

Dansen stood up and began to stammer his thanks. He wondered desperately if there was anything to add, any detail he had overlooked which might save Gran from herself, while he still had the attention of a Detective Inspector.

But it was Rushton, checking through the lines he had typed on his computer, who suddenly arrested his visitor's departure. "You say that you just missed Arthur

Rennie when he was round at your grandmother's house last Wednesday. You don't
mean yesterday, do you? You mean last
week: Wednesday, August 17th."

Dansen stopped on his way to the door.
"Yes. Is that date important?"

"It might be. Sit down again for a
moment."

The young man sat down as he was told,
undid the top button of the jacket he was
so unused to wearing, looked suddenly
anxious, as though he felt his evidence was
about to be questioned. Rushton studied
him for a moment, then smiled at the
worried face; in his own excitement, he
had forgotten the emotions of his inter-
viewee. "I'm not questioning anything
you've told me, Paul. It's just that the
time when Rennie was at your grandmother's house may be more important
than I thought at first. We're investigating
Arthur Rennie's possible involvement in
another, even more serious, crime and
he's given us an account of his whereabouts
on that evening which may conflict with
yours."

Paul Dansen did not make the connection
with the murder in the cathedral which
was dominating the newspapers, but he
caught a little of the older man's excitement. "He was at my gran's on that

Wednesday evening. I'd be prepared to swear to that."

Rushton smiled. "Don't be too ready to swear to it, Paul. You didn't see him there yourself, and from what you say of her I wouldn't like to put your gran in court as a witness."

Dansen bitterly voiced what Chris was thinking but had been reluctant to put into words. "She'll be dead before anything comes to court, anyway. But her neighbours saw Rennie in the house, when they came in to sign the will form. They could confirm the time when he left."

Rushton nodded. "What time did you get there yourself?"

"Quarter past nine. And Rennie had just gone. Gran said I'd just missed him. I think he passed me at the corner of the road in his car, but I couldn't be sure of that. He'd been there for about an hour; maybe a little less, but certainly not more, the neighbours said. I'm afraid I gave them rather a grilling, because I was annoyed that they'd put their names to the document as witnesses so easily. That wasn't fair really, because they didn't know who Rennie was and thought they were just helping Gran with a formality, being good neighbours."

Rushton's racing fingers put the information on to his computer. "We'll confirm this with your gran and her neighbours, in due course. But you'd say that Arthur Rennie was at your grandmother's house from around ten past eight until ten past nine on the evening of Wednesday, August 17th?"

"Certainly. I'll sign a statement to that effect, if you like." Paul Dansen didn't know what they could accuse Arthur Rennie of which was more serious than what the crook had done to his gran, but he felt the exhilaration of landing his first real blow on the man who had hitherto been so frustrating a quarry.

Chris Rushton saw Dansen out quickly. He was as eager as he had been ten year ago as a callow young DC to pass on his news. Arthur Rennie had not been at home as he had claimed on the night of his stepdaughter's murder. He had been swindling an old lady in the latter part of the evening, but before that he had enjoyed ample opportunity to kill his stepdaughter and deposit her body in the Lady Chapel. His alibi had just been blown to smithereens.

And so had that of Tamsin Rennie's witch of a mother.

Nineteen

"Try the hospitals, but try them last. My guess is that if you do have any success, it will be in an old people's home or a centre for the disabled. And give it priority; put three or four DCs on to it straight away." While Rushton was trying to put Paul Dansen at his ease at the beginning of their meeting, Lambert was giving urgent orders to another section of his team.

By the time Rushton came in excited with his news about the Rennies, Lambert had a result of his own. He held up his hand for a moment as he spoke on the phone. Russell, Baldwin and Bright, local estate agents, confirmed that the property was for sale and offered to send him the details. The Superintendent turned to his DI with an expression which Rushton found confident, and thus depressing; it meant his news was not going to have the impact he had expected and hoped for.

He plunged in nevertheless. "The young man who was put down by Arthur Rennie at his prayer meeting last night has turned up. He's given me the details of how his Gran was conned by Rennie. He's also been able to tell me where Rennie was at the time when his stepdaughter was murdered. And he wasn't at home, as he claimed."

"Good," said Lambert. "Very good work, Chris. It's time someone nailed the bugger. Follow it up. We should have enough on him now to get the details of his bank accounts, to find just where his money is coming from. When some of his donors find exactly what has been happening to their money, they'll be prepared to act as witnesses, I'm sure."

Lambert wasn't as good an actor as young Tom Clarke. Chris Rushton could tell his chief's mind was running on autopilot, that his real thoughts were elsewhere. He said, "You've got a breakthrough on this murder, haven't you, Guv'nor?" He relapsed into the copper's traditional form of address, a form not encouraged by Lambert and rarely used by his juniors, as if he was acknowledging that the two of them were just going through the motions.

"I think so, yes. I'm wondering how to set about proving it."

If Lambert was at the stage where he thought about the lawyers for the defence, about giving the Crown Prosecution Service a watertight case, then he was sure in his own mind who had done it, thought Chris. They might be at opposite ends of the CID continuum in many respects, but he had worked with this detective dinosaur long enough now to know the way his mind worked.

Lambert left Rushton with a series of phone calls to make and went out to the car where Bert Hook was already waiting in the driving seat. They were old hands at this game. Just like husband and wife, Christine Lambert and Eleanor Hook said when they compared notes and exchanged sympathy. They had been driving for some minutes before Bert said, "What put you on to it?"

Lambert did not smile. He had been trying to work out the very same thing himself: when had the first seed of suspicion been sown? Perhaps more important, when had it germinated in his dull mind? He stared unseeingly at the flying hedgerows as they drove on the road from Oldford to Hereford. "Did you ever read Sherlock Holmes as a lad?" he said unexpectedly.

Hook grinned. Typical of John Lambert to be oblique when you were screaming out for straight facts, whereas he was such a Gradgrind about facts and not opinions among his juniors. "Assemble all the relevant facts and the solution will be crystal clear," the Superintendent always told new members of his team. "Grub away at the facts, and only speculate when you are satisfied there are no more facts available to you." Now here he was talking about a fictional character who had operated a century earlier.

Bert played his part. Playing golf with the chief had taught him that even Lambert could be fallible. And ordinary, fallible people sometimes needed to be indulged. "I'm sure I did. But Dorothy L. Sayers was my adolescent favourite. When you were a lad living in a home, Lord Peter Wimsey and Oxbridge colleges were a world as different as that of a fairy tale."

"'Observation and deduction'," Lambert quoted, almost as if his sergeant had not spoken, thought Bert irritably. "Everyone can observe. It's what every young copper is taught to do, as soon as he enters the force. Deduction is more difficult. It's the difference between routine plodding and good CID work. Well, in the less straightforward cases, it is, anyway," he added defensively. "What I'm saying is that the vital thing was there for us all to observe. But it was placed within a thousand other details. Once you spot the right one, which is the difficult part, the deduction becomes easy."

He's getting worse, thought Bert. I'm sure as the old boy gets nearer to retirement, he's becoming more self-indulgent. But it's only when he relaxes, when he's got a result, so we might as well put up with it. And he was practical enough to set all the right things in motion before we left the station. The Drugs Squad is well aware of what we're about. The old fox is as careful of procedure as Chris Rushton, when he knows it's important.

At that moment, as if to confirm this thought, the radio buzzed with the news that the chief had been right to set his other inquiry in train before he left the station: the Leonard Cheshire Home had accepted the gift on the previous Friday evening.

It was almost four o'clock by the time Hook turned the car carefully into Rosamund Street. The sun was fully on the front of the house at this hour, making the newly painted front door of the Georgian house seem an even brighter blue, illuminating the normally shadowed steps down to the basement and the brass figures of 17a on the door of the flat where the ill-fated Tamsin Rennie had lived out the last months of her life.

Jane King opened the door no more than a foot. "It really isn't convenient. You should have rung before you came if—"

"If we wished to find the bird had flown when we arrived?" said Lambert fiercely. He pushed roughly past her, almost causing her to lose balance as she tried to hold the door against him, and strode into the ground-floor drawing room where they had talked to her on the two previous occasions. She followed him reluctantly, trapped between this suddenly belligerent man and the watchful Bert Hook, feeling as though she were already under arrest.

She stood facing them in the room, wondering if she could challenge this sudden entry into her house, noting that all three of them were breathing heavily, expectantly. It was a bizarre place for melodrama, this room with its tall Georgian windows looking out on the beds of salvias and geraniums beyond the green lawn. This garden could scarcely have changed since it was laid out two and a half centuries ago. She tried to think, to form some sort of plan, and found that her mind was not working with its normal swiftness under this sudden pressure.

That in itself was disconcerting. She must play for time; time to gather her resources, to try to assess how much they knew. Sugden might get her out of this, out of the country, somehow, if she could give him the time, if she could convince him that his own interests demanded it.

She said, "I suppose as you're here you'd better sit down," and did so abruptly, sending a shock through her own trunk with the forcefulness of her descent into the upright armchair. She could not even time her own physical movements now, she thought. She needed time to recover her poise and her thoughts, to organise her resistance to this confident assault.

She did not get it. Lambert sat down without taking his eyes from her face. "When did you clean the flat out?" he said.

"You mean the basement flat? The one where Tamsin—"

"You know what I mean."

"All right, then. The basement flat. Well, I suppose it was after your policemen had finished in there. The Scene of Crime team, you called them, I think. You said it would be all right to change the locks after they'd finished, and with the decorators waiting to start work I thought I'd better—"

"You cleaned it out before the Scene of Crime team got in there, didn't you? More than that, you removed whatever might incriminate you, left behind whatever you thought might lead us to other people."

Lambert had often felt sorry for murderers, when the hunt was over and they were safely in a cell. Many of the people he had taken for the gravest of all crimes had been pathetic rather than hateful, wandering out of their depth into stormy emotional

304

seas and floundering there. But not this time: he found himself wanting to grab this composed woman by the shoulders, to shake the truth out of her, to force her to contemplate the enormity of the crime she had planned and executed so calmly.

Jane King's outward calm held, though panic was racing within her, pounding the brain which had been so cool into hot confusion. She said foolishly, "I don't know what you mean. I asked you when I could move into the flat to clean it. I didn't go in there until then."

Lambert looked at her contemptuously. "If you insist on a string of lies, we might as well have them on record."

He nodded to Bert Hook, who stepped forward, put his hand lightly on the woman's shoulder, and said, "Jane King, I arrest you for the murder of Tamsin Elizabeth Rennie. You do not have to say anything, but it may harm your defence if you do not state material which may later be used in court. Anything you do say will be recorded and may be used in evidence against you." Without taking his eyes from her face, Hook resumed his seat on the edge of the chair opposite her, his face not more than six feet from hers, his notebook and ball-pen moving automatically into his hands.

The colour drained from her face with the formal words of arrest. But still she contrived somehow to keep the fear out of her widening blue eyes. She too was on the edge of her chair now, and Hook had the fantasy for a moment that her form, squat but trim in its tight-fitting blue sweater and navy trousers, might launch itself at one of them in a tigerish attack.

Lambert played his limited cards skilfully, striving to give the impression that they knew all about the background to this crime, that the whole of a vast drugs empire was being brought to heel at the same time as he was confronting Jane King with her crime. He said quietly, "Keith Sugden has been under investigation by our Drugs Squad for years. More to the point, from your point of view, his organisation has been infiltrated and his lines of communication have been revealed. We are ready to arrest the major players now, which is what we have been waiting for. You have helped to expose your particular section of the organisation by your murder of Tamsin Rennie."

"I don't know what you mean. Who on earth is this Keith Sugden you're trying to make so much of?"

But she had started on the name when it was mentioned, and four watchful eyes had noted that. Lambert went on as if she had not spoken, "Your crime was useless, you see, as an attempt to conceal your involvement as a supplier. It will, however, secure you a life sentence for murder, as well as whatever you are given for supplying drugs." He spoke as if that thought gave him great satisfaction.

The brittle calm which King had preserved shattered with the mention of a life sentence. Her face now white as paper, she spoke harshly, as though the phrases were wrung from deep within her by some agency beyond her control. "I had no alternative. That little tart was going to betray us. She knew the score, knew I couldn't just let her walk out of here. Stupid bitch!"

"Tamsin was going to give up working as a supplier, to go for a cure and inform on the drugs world you'd got her into."

He made it a statement, not a question; it was a guess, but the only one that fitted the facts. Jane King said with a flash of her old contempt, "She'd got herself into it. Once they're addicts, they don't have a choice, do they? She needed her fix twice a day, and eventually the only way she could pay for that was by agreeing to peddle coke and smack for us. Of course she said she was going to give up, they always do. When you tell them what the cure involves, they can't

face the throwing up, the sweats, the consti-
pation followed by the shits. They just reach
for the next fix. At a hundred and fifty
pounds a gram for smack, that costs."

"But some do manage to come off smack.
Just a few, with help. The heroin clinics
have a high percentage of success, once
they get people in there. And if they know
where their supplies are coming from, as
Tamsin Rennie did, cured addicts mean
trouble for people like you."

The bright blue eyes glittered with hatred
as she glared at him, and he knew now that
he had convinced her that he knew the
whole of this. King said bitterly, "She said
this time she was going to go away with that
actor fellow, to get married eventually, she
hoped. Stupid little tart! She said she'd
keep her mouth shut about what she'd been
doing and where she'd got the gear from,
but I knew she wouldn't. Not when you lot
got at her."

"And so you killed her. And it's all for
nothing."

She started half to her feet on that, as
though she would spring upon him with her
nails flailing. Hook abandoned his short-
hand and prepared to restrain her, but
Lambert moved not a fraction, his chin jut-
ting aggressively at her, his lined face full of
what seemed a real loathing. She sank back

upon her chair. In a low voice, she said, "There was no other way. And that man, that maniac they called the Sacristan, made me think I might add her to his list of victims. I knew I could get her into the Cathedral, because of the choir rehearsal. She'd told me about that herself, because she was so proud of her idiot boyfriend being in it."

"But you didn't kill her there. She died here."

There was no attempt at concealment now. Only an awful smirk at the recollection. "She died in the chair you're sitting in. She was trying to get me to join her in coming clean, as she called it. Stupid little bitch. I tried to tell her that neither of us could do that, that she was committed to us now, whether she liked it or not, but she was full of this new life she was going to have. I got her up here and pretended I'd just come in from the garden, walked up behind her as she sat where you are. I pretended to be caressing her neck, massaging her as part of my persuasion not to do what she was threatening. She was too busy anticipating the fix she was due to take much notice of what my hands were doing, until it was too late. I just squeezed, and kept on squeezing. She died in less than a minute, I should think. Without even a sound!"

There was an awful pride in her handi-work; she seemed unable to prevent herself from piling detail upon detail, once she started, as if this single act of murderous violence had now a fascination for her. Lambert, usually loath to interrupt any confession, was actually glad to terminate her account of what had happened in this quiet room. He said evenly, "So you had a corpse in this chair, which you had to get into the Lady Chapel of the Cathedral."

"Yes. And you don't know how I did that." For an instant, satisfaction stole back into her square face, as if she had forgotten her situation.

Then Lambert said, "Oh, but we do, Mrs King. That was your first mistake, though it took me too long to see it for that. The wheelchair was in the hall when we first came here, though you'd dispensed with it by the time we came back on Tuesday. Incidentally, we've checked with your tenants: none of them had had a visit from a disabled relative, as you claimed."

The blue eyes narrowed. She was shaken even further by their knowledge of the wheelchair. This lean, intense opponent seemed to have discovered everything. She dropped now into the expression of low cunning both experienced men had often seen on the faces of not very intelligent

310

petty thieves. "I don't know what you mean, wheelchair. You'll have to prove there was such a thing here."

Lambert smiled. "The wheelchair was recovered from the Leonard Cheshire home this morning: it hadn't yet been used there. It's on its way to our forensic laboratories now. I've no doubt they'll find some traces of Tamsin Rennie or her clothes upon it." He looked into the frustrated, vicious face opposite him, seeking only for some way to keep it speaking. "It was an ingenious method of getting a body to the Cathedral: I'll admit that."

She responded immediately. "That idiot actor came here, just after I'd killed his stupid girlfriend. I heard him shouting to her through the letter box. He called out that he couldn't hang about, that he had to go to his choir rehearsal. Then he used his key to get into the flat. When I heard him go, I gave him a few minutes, then got the girl's body into the wheelchair, with a head-scarf round the head. No one looks at a person in a wheelchair, you know. I once followed Peter Ustinov right through the exit route at Heathrow, and because he was in a wheelchair, no one looked at him and no one recognised him. I pushed her along St Ethelbert Street without anyone giving us a second look — not that there was anyone much about at that time."

"Not even at the Cathedral, I imagine."

She shook her head with a quick, mirth-less smile. She seemed almost detached, so full was she of her own cunning in those moments. "They were just beginning the choir rehearsal. I could hear them as I reached the St John's door at the back of the Cathedral, which had been left open to allow them in. I only got the idea of the Lady Chapel when I got inside. It was the one place I could get to easily, without being seen by the people at the rehearsal."

"And no doubt you had plenty of time to arrange her upon the altar."

"Yes. I found a sign about work in progress, saying that people should not go beyond it, and I put that outside the entrance to the Lady Chapel, just in case anyone should come along. I tried to remember how the Sacristan had laid out his victims in those country churches. I put her on the steps of the altar, between two big candlesticks, and folded her hands on her breast, as he had done. Like the figure on the tomb at the side of the Chapel. I even combed her hair back to imitate that."

But you couldn't simulate the Sacristan's sexual assaults upon his victims, thought Lambert, or you might have had this killing pinned on him for a while longer. He found

312

he had an almost personal need to deflate this creature, who seemed to so relish her dispatch of a young life. "You didn't deceive us, you know, not beyond the first few hours."

He had thought she would want to know the reason why. Instead, she said curiously, "What made you suspect me? I knew you'd go to the parents, that you'd find them a suspect and interesting pair. And I left enough in the flat to give you others to follow up when I went through it."

He shrugged. "A variety of things. We found you'd arrived at your friends' house for dinner an hour later than you claimed at our first meeting, as I reminded you. You told our Scene of Crime team that Tamsin Rennie was 'a clean and tidy girl' when you were offering them nothing else in the way of information: that was always very unlikely for a smack addict. And you were always the likeliest person to have cleared the flat. You had your own entry to the place from the main part of the house, so that you could get in there any time you wanted."

She said, like one taking pride in her work, "I went through the place late on the Wednesday night after I'd taken the body to the Cathedral and been out to my friends' house for dinner. Cleaned it very thoroughly. Put all the slut's clothes away, removed all traces of myself and the supplies of snow and smack I'd given her to sell."

"And you left the two photographs, very obvious clues that would lead us quite certainly to other people. They were regular visitors, with their pictures in her flat; people you would have known about, but you pretended not to know about them when we first talked to you, because you knew you'd left us the photographs for us to follow up."

"I knew you'd get to young Clarke, but it would have been odd if there wasn't at least one picture of the boyfriend, so I decided to leave the one in that poncy actor's pose. And I thought you might not even get on to Councillor bloody Whittaker unless I left his picture for you. He came round and tried to get into the flat, you know, the next night, but I'd put the catch on from the inside. I heard him trying the door when I was going to bed, but his key wouldn't let him in." She smiled with satisfaction as she thought of that sad man's frustration.

"And when we came to see you, you could afford to pretend you had little knowledge of them, to drone on about the privacy of your tenants."

She seemed to resent this as a slur on her

tactics, to have become unconscious of her situation in her desire to emphasise her own ingenuity. "I talked about them when you came the second time."

"Indeed. You were markedly more forthcoming about other suspects when we interviewed you for a second time, which made me think you were concerned we might investigate you more fully."

"You were talking more about drugs by then, as though they might be connected with her death."

"And you were scared. I noticed the estate agent's literature on your table when we spoke, though you tried to give me the impression it was there just because you wanted to re-let Tamsin Rennie's flat. I now know that you have put this house on the market, though there is no agent's board outside. You were planning to get out, Mrs King."

"Yes. Well, I was right, wasn't I? I should have gone more quickly, that's all. McDonald might at least have told me you were close."

Neither of the two men even blinked as Hook wrote down the name. It was a new one to them, one she thought they already possessed, presumably the next one up in the chain from her in the carefully hidden line that led eventually to Keith Sugden at the head of his billion-pound criminal enterprise. If Jane King thought they knew everything, so much the better. Her indiscretions might save a few other Tamsin Rennies from violent deaths.

Jane King had not referred to the dead girl by name throughout their exchanges. She did not even glance down the steps to the flat as they led her out of her house.

Lambert drove the car out of Rosamund Street, whilst Jane King sat handcuffed to Hook on the back seat. They were almost out in the countryside before they caught a glimpse of the great tower of Hereford Cathedral, standing sentinel over the old city as it had done for centuries.

Later the next evening, Lambert handed in the tickets he had secured two months earlier at the door of Hereford Cathedral. Then he sat next to Christine and heard the voices of Tom Clarke and his two hundred companions soaring exultantly towards the high ceiling above the nave of the Cathedral in Elgar's *Dream of Gerontius*.

And John Lambert wondered how many other minds kept coming back, like his, to the Lady Altar, invisible to them all from where they sat, where the bizarre scene which had dominated his life for the last nine days had been set out like a pagan sacrifice in this Christian place.